A Rose for William Carter

By

Gerald Harding Gunn

ISBN 978-0615758404

For Lois

A ROSE FOR WILLIAM CARTER

A Rose for William Carter

The house, chalky white and faded among the bare limbed oaks that stood in the front yard, was a ghost of itself at the end of the red mud road. It looked sullen, abandoned, not the way Aunt Lucille would have wanted, but she was dead now; two weeks in her grave in Elam at the 1st Methodist Church. William did not want to be there, did not want to see the house shrouded in its winter veil, made doubly cold by her absence and the knowing that she would never return.

Aunt Lucille was his favorite and William loved her. She was not his aunt by blood, but had become like a sister to his mother Ellie Carter after they formed a loving friendship when they began teaching together at Elam Elementary School a year before William was born.

"Lord, would you look at who's come out here to see me? Come here boy!" she would cry out when he arrived, emerging from his parent's Buick in khaki shorts and bleached T-shirt, his feet clad in white canvas sneakers. She would rush toward him, freckled arms open to surround him and hold him and hug him and rescue him from the drudging boredom of summer life back in Elam.

"You get in here, I got some baked cookies that need eating up and fresh milk that needs drinking. "Ellie, you tryin' to starve this child, he ain't nothin' but skin and bones."

Momma would break out in a grin and accuse Lucille of trying to fatten up her only child so much she would have to buy him bigger clothes.

His cousin Kelsey Carter's voice was a rasp, a piece of hard, naked chalk, raking across his memory, erasing the pleasant day of years ago when the sun caressed Aunt 'Cille's house and warmed his childhood. "What cha' grinnin' at Willie Boy?" Kelsey smirked.

"Nothing, just remembering, just a thought," William replied.

"You remember too much, boy, but then you damn Elam Carters always remember too much, especially you, Professor Carter, but then your business is rememberin' ain't it," Kelsey said. "Well, there's the driveway." Kelsey lit another cigarette, his sixth since he picked William up in his crumpled, dirty Ford F-100 pickup for the trip out to Aunt Cille's house.

The truck pulled into the driveway, slamming to a stop in front of the walkway. Kelsey's bulging hulk was wrapped in a soiled woolen CPO jacket. He hopped out and as he walked up the steps to the front door he fumbled for the key, the cigarette hanging from plump lips surrounded by a three-day-old beard.

William looked at his fat cousin. He congratulated himself on his resolve to lose weight, working out, jogging, finally controlling his diet and getting trim, toning himself into his present shape, a shape that suited his five foot, six inch frame.

Kelsey's remaining hair was now heavily flecked with gray, and William had noticed some silver in his own mirror reflection recently while shaving.

"Well, come on Professor Willie, this is your party, let's get this done, I ain't got all day", he said, unlocking the door.

William knew it was no use to remind his cousin that he did not like the nickname. He would only use it more to harass and aggravate. Something Kelsey had gleefully, spitefully done since they were children.

From Kelsey the title 'professor' sounded like an insult, as if he resented someone who was educated and chose to impart knowledge. Aunt 'Cille always called him William...she never called him Willie.

The cousins from the 'Bottom' always called Aunt 'Cille "Cille". They would deliberately pronounce it, 'SEE-UL', a mark of disrespect that Momma said characterized the Carters from East Mim County. "You always call her Aunt Lucille, or if she lets you, Aunt 'Cille, but I better never hear you call her 'Cille like those 'Bottom' Carters," Momma would tell him.

The aroma of her life greeted them and deepened William's longing and sadness when Kelsey unlocked the front door and opened it. Hints of home cooking, her personal scent, the slight staleness of her many old books, all drifted up to them saying, "*Lucille Carter lived here...her home... her place was here.*"

"Damn, smells kinda musty in here," was Kelsey's only reaction.

William thought the observation did not deserve a reply. He intended to say as little as possible to one of those who treated his aunt badly in life, and would not show her any kindness or respect after her death. The house did not smell musty to him.

"Where'd you say that thing was?" Kelsey queried, "I ain't plannin' to spend the whole day out here huntin' for it."

"It's in the bedroom," William replied, "unless someone has moved it."

"Well now, nobody's moved it, it's still there safe and sound, don't you worry Willie. I've been out here to have a look around, but nobody's touched nothin'... course, it ain't gonna stay that way long."

Lucille Carter's presence still possessed her most private room, where she read, sewed, thought, prayed and died. "Died of a heart attack, right there, she did," Kelsey said, entering the bedroom and looking down at the bed, unchanged since the moment her visiting friend, Lillian Scott, found her after entering the house.

William stared at the bed and the room. He had not seen it since her death. And in all his visits in childhood and later after he was grown and came from Elam to visit, he had only been in the room a handful of times. It was a place where Aunt 'Cille wanted to be alone, she had never forbade him entry, but he had sensed he did not belong there and rarely entered.

On her bedside table was a framed ambro-type image of a clean-shaven man, a cravat tied at the base of his neck, wearing a black broadcloth coat.

Time had yellowed the exposure made before there were film cameras. Most of the old pictures he had seen in museums and other places showed stern, determined faces and he had read people at that time considered photography a solemn occasion, not a time for a warmer expression which they considered frivolous. Having your picture taken back then was also a bit of a chore, since you had to hold your pose for a long time, and could not move because of the nature of the exposure. That alone would discourage anyone from looking cheerful.

William often imagined why this dark haired man had a faint smile, why his eyes, he guessed they were blue from their light tint, seemed to stare gently, almost lovingly. Was it because he wanted someone he greatly cared for to know that he cared? Was this his way of bidding farewell? Of saying, "I am going away, but will return soon, so I am leaving you my smile behind to remember me by?" Aunt 'Cille said she did not know, or would not say. "His name was William Carter, same as yours, but you ain't named for him. Your Momma just liked the name William. Someday you will learn about him" was all she ever said about the man in the oval frame.

"Well, I reckon that's it, right there," Kelsey observed, pointing to the trunk at the foot of the bed. "That's what you said she wanted you to have, so let's get it out to the truck."

The trunk was brown and old and heavy, and Kelsey grumbled about its weight all the way from the bedroom to the truck bed.

Outside it felt colder as the day wore on to early afternoon, and the gray sky overhead looked heavy laden. "Wish this cold snap would let up, looks like we're in for another dose of froze up stuff...ice, maybe snow this time, so I'm gettin' you and your trunk back to town," Kelsey said, glancing up at the clouds. "I'm gonna go back and lock the door, then let's go."

William nodded and silently re-entered the truck. Kelsey lit up another cigarette, puffing smoke that blew over the steering wheel and into the windshield. "Picked a real nice day to go souvenir collecting, Willie boy," he said, "but I guess today was as good as any other. I gotta get Jake Kelso out here to appraise this place, hope by Monday, if this damn weather lets up."

William stared straight ahead and watched the gray horizon grow darker as it met the mud road and its ice that refused to melt. "What are you going to do with her things?" he asked.

Kelsey, pretending not to pay attention, tossed his butt out the window and lit a fresh one as the truck approached the paved main road to town. "What'd you say?"

William shifted slightly on the seat, knowing it would do no good to ask Kelsey to roll down the window slightly to let the smoke escape. He had tried cigarettes only once, they made him sick, and he hated the smell.

"I said what are you going to do with her things?" raising his voice enough so that Kelsey could hear him and could not ignore him.

"I figured you'd get around to asking that sooner or later." Kelsey flicked an ash on the floorboard and took another deep drag.

"Well, that ain't really none of your business, but I'll tell you anyway. I'm gonna sell every damn bit of it that will sell, and chuck out the rest, but I figure there's enough old stuff that folks might be interested in who like to buy it and collect it. I can pretty well do as I please with it...you know that, 'cause I'm entitled. Cille wanted you to have that damned old trunk, God knows why, don't know why she did not leave any more of the stuff to you or your side, but she didn't and that's that."

William felt his pulse rising because of this man... this ugly, hateful man...his kin by blood, but no kin otherwise, but he knew what Kelsey was expecting him to say, so he said something different.

"Kelsey, I want to thank you for driving me out here today, in spite of the weather, to get Aunt 'Cille's trunk. I don't really know why she wanted me to have it either, but as you said, she did, and that's that, but I will cherish it, care for it, see what is inside of it and preserve and protect whatever it is. Kelsey, I know that you and your side of the Carters did not care for Aunt 'Cille like I did, but before you dispose of the rest of her belongings, could you consider holding on to them, for the family's sake? Once things like that are gone, they are gone for good and you can't get them back."

Kelsey shook his head, and then lit another smoke as the truck passed the Elam city limit sign and headed down Mim Avenue to William's house. "Don't care where they go and don't want them back. Now you hear this and hear it good 'cause I ain't gonna repeat it, Willie. That old woman never gave a damn for any of us, you'd a thought she could have been at least civil after Daddy let her stay on the place, but what did she do, she took it over like she owned it and treated us all like dirt. That's the way it's been since I was a kid, and you high and mighty Elam Carters treated us the same way, damn you all. Well here's news for you; I didn't have to carry you out there today to pick up that damn trunk, but I did and while I reckon I ought to acknowledge your thanks for it, I don't give a damn whether you thank me or not. I got a right to everything that's out there. Daddy left me the land, I'm gonna sell it and make money and that's more important than hanging on to a bunch of old crap."

Kelsey slammed on the brakes in front of William's home. "Well, here we are...got one more thing to make clear Willie. That old clap trap house and the fifty or so acres it sits on is becoming Mim County's new subdivision in a few months, quick as I make the sale and make the money. Let's just get you and your precious trunk off my truck, I've wasted enough time."

Large, mushy white flakes began to drift down from the gunmetal sky and cover the ground and the street. "Damn...was counting on seeing Jake today and setting up things for Monday, guess that will have to wait, thanks to you," Kelsey said as he lowered the tailgate and began pulling the trunk out. "You better give me a hand unless you want me to just drop it on the street."

William grabbed the trunk as Kelsey slid it out, taking its full weight. "I've got it, and again, thanks for your time Kelsey. I'm sorry I inconvenienced you today, I can see you've got a lot on your mind."

"Well, all that muscle all of a sudden, Haw!" Kelsey said, as he let go and stood back. "Ever the gentleman, ain't ya? 'Thanks for your time, sorry to inconvenience', he says...Haw!" Kelsey lit up again, wadding up the empty pack and throwing it on the ground, breaking out another as he got back behind the wheel and cranked the motor. "See you around Willie boy."

Kelsey drove away, the truck's slick rear tires skidding on the snowy pavement. William waited until the truck was gone before he put the trunk down, determined that Kelsey would see him holding it, denying the pain in his arms from the strain of its weight. He let it down as gently as he could, trying not to drop it in the snow. Actually, the snow helped in a way; he was able to slide the trunk to the front steps, then, pausing for a breath, he calculated his next move; how to get the thing up the steps and to the door.

It was a steamer style trunk with a hinged, rounded top that permitted its owner to fill the square body and put more and more in until hopefully all one's possessions were tucked and stuffed inside.

William's arms still ached from the effort, and he thought of the men who loaded the steamboats, ships and trains and who had to contend with hundreds of these behemoths every day. It sat at the base of the steps as if daring him to heft it again, but with the snow mantle steadily growing thicker, he knew somehow he had to move it inside.

The snow and the increasing cold reminded him he needed to move inside as well. Leather straps braced the trunk on its left and right, and William gripped them and pulled, hoping time and age would not cause them to give way and snap. He feared he would slip on the steps, that the trunk would fall back, break open in the snow, and its contents, whatever it was Aunt 'Cille intended for him to have and to see would be damaged, possibly lost for good. So he mustered himself, focused and strained, and the trunk, slowly at first, began to move up the steps.

William would have given anything for a helping hand behind the trunk pushing up and halfway, he was afraid he would lose his grip, but he kept pulling, pulling, telling himself don't let up, don't let up, and the trunk gave up the struggle and found itself level and on the porch. He paused for another breath, a longer pause this time and was glad he did not smoke.

"That damned Kelsey couldn't have done what I just did," he said to the trunk. "All right my old friend... let's get out of the cold."

Chapter 2

William unlocked the front door and stood inside for a moment, the warmth of the house a welcome relief from the weather outside, then, leaving the door open, he brushed the snow off the trunk, dragged it across the threshold into the living room and closed the door to shut out the chill.

The message indicator on his phone was blinking as he expected it would be, and he pressed the playback button. "You could have let me know you were going somewhere", her recorded message scolded. "With this weather coming in I've been worried; call me when you get home." There were other messages, he ignored them and returned the call from the scolding voice.

"Hi," William said when he heard her answer, "Just got back from Aunt 'Cille's. Whatever she left me, whatever she wanted me to have and save is in an old steamer trunk that is now sitting in my living room. I want you to see it with me Bobbie...wouldn't ask anyone else. Come on over."

"And why should I do that," she answered. "You didn't bother to let me know you'd be gone most of the day or where you were going. Have you taken a look outside in the past few minutes, we're in a snow storm, hell, a blizzard, and here I was worried you got caught in it, and now you want me to get out and get caught in it! You're a scoundrel William Carter! I'll be right there."

Curiosity killed the cat...William hoped it would not kill Roberta Grace Cribbs as she drove her Jeep CJ through the thickening snow to his house. She did not have far to travel, just two blocks, and he knew she could drive in bad weather.

"You're a scoundrel, William Carter!" she said, and William cracked a smile recalling her remark. Roberta (Bobbie) Cribbs was a scoundrel as well, in her own way, which is why he loved her so much, ever since they first met.

She had thrown a rock at him in the third grade at Elam Elementary School and was escorted to the principal's office for it, but as the school years passed and they both emerged as high school freshmen, oddly, it struck him, her attitude seemed to change, but then, his feelings about her began to change too.

He had been the victim of her distain and pranks during all their growing up in Elam, but it was one prank, maybe not intended as a prank, that had drawn them together. He had met whom he regarded as the 'true' Roberta, the woman he loved, on a dating service site, under a different name, of course. He had corresponded via email with 'Julia', a schoolteacher who said she lived in Elam. Julia appealed to him, learning that she had the same likes and dislikes, a love of history and family, and love for camping and hiking and nature, a love for teaching, a love of books and so they agreed to meet and have dinner.

William was excited and somewhat nervous, not really knowing what to expect, since 'Julia' had never sent him her picture, though he had sent his to her. He had invited her to the best after hours restaurant in Elam, the 'Lark Nest'. She said she knew the place and warmly accepted his invitation. He arrived on time, shortly before six, to find Roberta Cribbs sitting in the lobby.

He had not seen her in a while, she looked different, much more appealing than the last time he had seen her shortly after she had come back to Elam to teach after her University of Georgia graduation. She was nicely dressed, must be waiting on a date, he thought.

"Well, hi there, Bobbie," he said. "So nice to see you, how have you been? Guess you're waiting on some nice guy to buy you dinner."

"I've been waiting on you, William Carter," she replied. "You see, Julia is my pen name, and I have been waiting on a nice guy to buy me dinner, and that nice guy is you. Looks like you have fallen prey to me again, kiddo, hope you won't be sore, 'cause I'm hungry."

William felt he had a right to be sore, but this was the gal he had put up with nearly all his life, at first hated, then liked, and was now beginning to be deeply in love with in spite of himself. He could not resist cracking a smile.

"You're a scoundrel, Roberta Cribbs", he exclaimed, and they both burst out laughing. "Come on, let's eat."

He heard the Jeep pull up, its windshield wipers whipping the white accumulation off the glass. The front door flew open and quickly closed, and a scarfed, slender female figure in blue denim and hiking boots yanked off the scarf and a wool toboggan cap, turned to him and said, "You better have some hot coffee going in that kitchen." Her hair fell long and full down her back when she pulled off the cap, rushing down in an auburn wave. "Oh! You're impossible!" she shouted as she met his arms and they held each other tightly, moist lips caressing in a lingering kiss. "I am not seeking affection, it's cold as a tomb in here, turn up the heat and get a fire going in case the power fails again," and then she fell silent.

She stared at the trunk, its ancient brownness and rounded top held her attention for a long moment. "Ma Cribbs had one like that," she said, the trunk still holding her focus. "After she passed, I was there when Uncle Seth and Aunt Helen opened it. All they found was old newspaper clippings and some of her old clothes and that was about it. That took care of the old rumor that Ma had gold coins hidden away in it. They took everything out and went through it over and over...no coins," Bobbie snickered.

"But you told me they did find coins, a lot of them, you wound up with a couple of them," William recalled from the kitchen as he started a pot of coffee perking.

"Oh, yeah, they found them months later in an old shoe box inside her bedroom chest of drawers. Uncle Seth and Aunt Helen and Momma divided them up among the grandkids, we each got two of them," Bobbie replied as she unbuttoned her denim jacket and placed it on the sofa. "And there was a wad of Confederate bills; nobody wanted them but me. I saved them, still plan to frame them some day."

"It's finally warming up in here, I heard the heat cut on, but I'd still like a fire William Carter, so get cracking" Bobbie chided. "Then we'll see what Aunt 'Cille saved for you."

"Well, how about the coffee first Miss Cribbs?" William moved from the kitchen counter with two cups filled with the liquid, steaming and fragrant, and Bobbie accepted hers, and began sipping it.

"Ummm, good old Eight O'Clock. I just might forgive you after all or dragging me out on a day like this."

Bobbie glanced out the window. "Lord, look at it, it's falling harder now, four incher, maybe five, Elam's going to get snowed in tonight. Looks like I'm going to get snowed in with you and this trunk of yours. I don't see a fire in the fireplace yet, William Carter."

The wind was blowing the snow up on the porch, a thick white coating had already made the front steps invisible and Bobbie's Jeep was barely recognizable. As Bobbie had reminded him, the ice storm that struck Elam and Mim County earlier in the week had cut the power for two days, leaving homes without heat. William had made up his mind not to get caught unprepared a second time, and made sure he had a plentiful supply of kindling and dry wood for the fireplace in case the weather shut off the electricity again.

"It must be years and years old," Bobbie said as she turned her attention back to the trunk. William struck a long stemmed match and ignited the kindling he had placed on the fireplace grate. "The trunk itself might be pretty valuable, it's undoubtedly late nineteenth Century...possibly early twentieth...but I think it's older."

Bobbie placed her coffee cup on the lamp table next to the couch and kneeled beside the trunk. She started softly caressing it, moving her fingers across its surface roughened by age, and then she touched the latch. "Ma's trunk had a latch like this. Uncle Seth started to pry it open with a screw driver and then Aunt Helen wiggled it just a little and it just fell open."

Bobbie pressed the latch just slightly, and it released and dropped down. She looked up at William and smiled. "Open Sesame! It fell almost by itself, as if it wanted to. William, I'm not going to open it; that's for you to do. Now, I'm not superstitious but I've got the feeling just now that Aunt 'Cille wants you to look inside."

William placed his cup next to Bobbie's and sat down on the couch; Bobbie slowly stood and then sat down beside him. She took his hand and they stared at the trunk as it silently invited them to open its rounded, arched top. The kindling in the fireplace flickered to life. William broke the silence.

"Looks like it's time to put a log on your fire...get it going for you," he said. William added more kindling and then placed a seasoned log on top, the oak began to burn and its scent drifted from the hearth.

"That's more like it," Bobbie said. "Now quit fiddling with the fire and open this thing."

William thought the top would be heavy, recalling how he struggled to get the trunk inside the house, but it did not resist him. "Calico...two bolts of it, and it looks like it's new!" Bobbie exclaimed. William remembered that Aunt 'Cille made her own dresses and his summer clothes when he saw the bright material. "There's enough to make a dress or two, it's amazing the condition it's in, after all this time."

Bobbie lifted the brown bolt of calico and stroked it, admiring it with her fingers, holding it up to the table lamp, fascinated. "Wonder how old it is? Oh, William, it's lovely, I wish I could have it."

William smiled. "Well, I don't sew; bet you could make a warm weather dress out of it, maybe a blouse, or an apron. Consider it your gift from Aunt 'Cille."

"Do you mean it William? Oh thank you! You are hereby forgiven for enticing me out into this blizzard." She placed the calico on the table, slid over beside him and touched his face and then his lips with hers. "Well, William Carter, I have my gift from Aunt 'Cille, let's look further and find yours."

William wondered why his aunt wanted him to have this relic, why this? There were any number of things he would have been happy with to remember her by. Why this thing containing bits and pieces of her life? He had wondered ever since she told him she wanted him to have the trunk a year ago, just saying he would find it held things of value and truth.

The calico fabric was contained in a drawer that spanned the top section of the trunk and now he lifted it out. A Sears Roebuck Consumers Guide met the light. Age had made the pages crisp, but they were still firm and the still colorful cover in bright red, green and yellow proclaimed Sears as "The Cheapest Supply House on Earth, Our trade reaches around the World."

"Care to order something?" William grinned as he handed the catalog to Bobbie, who was still admiring the calico. Bobbie grinned back and began thumbing through it. "Hmmm, let's see, ladies wear starts on page 676 with hats, I'm sure I'll find something snappy. There's everything but the kitchen sink in here...oh wait, kitchen sinks are on page 921," she laughed. "What else do you see?"

The next item he saw was a copy of the Gospel Primer that had seen much use. Aunt 'Cille as a child had scrawled her name in cursive inside the front cover; "Lucille Carter, 1922." When new it had a scrolled pattern cover, a blending of pastel orange and green, at its center was a pen and ink drawing of Jesus with the children, illustrating the passage, *Suffer the little children to come unto me.*" William thumbed through it and saw that it taught basic arithmetic and English, and contained a list of stories based on scripture from the Old and New Testaments. "They learned the Bible along with their basic math and letters," William said, handing it to Bobbie.

"Sure did; don't imagine a book like this would show up in the schools these days," she said. Aunt 'Cille's black leather bound Bible emerged next, with its cover cracked and brittle, but the binding was firm, still holding the pages in place.

"Lucille Joanna Carter" was clearly legible in gold leaf in the lower right hand corner. Dog-eared pages and church bulletins had helped her find her favorite passages, which were carefully underlined in black ink. When William turned to Proverbs a string bound packet slipped out and dropped to the floor, falling from Page 916 where she had underlined Verse 29 in the 11th Chapter. *"He that troubleth his own house shall inherit the wind...and the fool shall be servant to the wise of heart."*

Bobbie picked up the packet and handed it to him. "Letters...it's a packet of letters," she said. "Looks like you have found a treasure, maybe your gift. Wonder who wrote them, they look very old. I've got that feeling again William, the way they sort of fell out, almost on their own, like she wanted to call your attention to them, like she left them for you to see."

Dark had fallen on Elam, but outside the snow cover made everything appear luminous and unearthly. The corner streetlight shone down on a scene with obliterated features, as if someone had dumped a giant box of laundry powder on the town. William was grateful to be inside, and although he could not feel it, he sensed the cold. He turned from the window. Bobbie was sitting on the couch, holding the packet.

"How about some more coffee?" he asked.

"Could use some", she said. "Why did you get up just now, like something made you restless?"

William picked up their cups and walked into the kitchen. He poured more steaming liquid into the cups from the percolator. "I don't know...a little excited, a little skittish maybe. Could be there is something written there I don't want to see, but as you say, it looks like she meant for me to see them."

William walked back to the trunk and loosened the string that had held the letters together, binding them to each other for so many years in the bottom of the trunk. Aunt 'Cille must have taken care that the trunk was kept in a dry place so that no moisture ever touched it. The paper was dry and yet not brittle. The trunk then was a time capsule, cradling its contents, preserving what normally would have vanished or at least been distorted beyond recognition. On the back of each letter she had penned the names Joanna and William in bold cursive.

"Who were they?" Bobbie asked. "Do you know them...distant ancestors maybe?"

"Aunt 'Cille was named for Joanna, that's her middle name," William replied. "Joanna Carter would have been my great, great aunt. She never spoke much about her, just told me once she died sadly, that death for her was a blessing. She was John Carter's wife. I learned that on my own while researching local Civil War regiments. He was a member of the Elam Guards, which became Company 'G' of the 67th Georgia Regiment that fought against Sherman. The 67th fought a skirmish against a federal cavalry patrol near the house. All Aunt 'Cille ever told me was that there was fighting there, but never talked much about that either. John and Joanna lived there and John literally wound up fighting on his own land, defending his own place."

"They actually won a victory that day, a hollow one, since Sherman's armies had already turned the Confederate flank again and moved down toward Cobb County and Marietta. After the battle, a patrol from Company 'G' found John and Joanna dead at the house. According to the company commander's report, they were killed by Yankees retreating from the battle, probably in revenge for their men who were killed."

"I wonder who he wrote these to?" Bobbie asked as she picked up one of William Carter's letters.

William took the letter from her and held it. "Who knows?" he replied. "There was a William Carter in Company 'G' who was one of the original Elam Guards when they mustered in 1862. He was listed as missing in action during the fighting in this area, I think...and that's all anyone knew. I believe he was related to John... I think they were cousins."

William opened the envelope and it revealed a crumpled rectangular paper and a brief message in pencil. The writer had used the back of a cartridge wrapper and the wrapper still had the arsenal mark: *"Ten Cartridges for Enfield Rifle or Rifle Musket, Cal.57, Augusta Arsenal, May 1864."* William Carter suffered the deficiency of most Confederate troops writing home, that of a shortage of paper. They had to make do with what they could find or improvise, and a cartridge wrap's reverse and blank side was plentiful and handy.

William began to feel something he had sensed before when going over old letters and diaries; time transformation, going back to the actual moment when the writer composed his message to someone who cared about what was happening to him. Bobbie interrupted his thoughts. "Hey, you still here?" she said, smiling.

"It's a note, written on a piece of cartridge wrapper, looks like Confederate issue, written shortly after the Battle of Resaca, about mid-May 1864."

Joanna, my love,

God protect you. The federals may be moving toward Mim County soon. Go to Elam, you will be safer there. I must talk to John. Pray for me, pray for us both.

William read it aloud to her. "It's signed, simply... William."

William removed a letter with Joanna's name on the envelope, unfolded it, and began to read it to Bobbie as the hearth fire glowed, and the snow continued to blow against the windows.

Elam, June 1,'64

Dearest William,

I pray you are well. The News that reaches Elam tells me the war is approaching. With so many dead at Resaca, I thank our merciful God you are spared. How long will it be until I see you again? I miss you so. Dear God, I am in agony. I long for your touch, your taste and your scent upon me, your precious smile glowing down at me, your precious essence flowing into me.

It has been too long, too long, since our time in February when you had furlough and came to me, since your caress, the sweetness, the joy of our joining, our closeness, when I felt you deep within me, when we were one in our love, forbidden, but God, so glorious!

I wish somehow you could appear to me now, this moment that we could just disappear to Florida, to Texas, to Mexico, anywhere and leave this unhappy, frightful world behind. The photographer's image of you is all I have to remind me of your smile and I treasure it at my bedside every night. Your expression is so loving. William, what shall we do, I now carry your child, not his.

We are bound to John Carter by kinship, by blood, but for me, not by love. He is so cold, you are like sunshine, my sunshine.

Please stay safe and whole for me.

Joanna

Chapter 3

Elam, 1864

The snow had begun to fall on Elam as William followed Joanna from church, the words of Reverend Hezekiah Crawford still echoed in the sanctuary.

"We beseech thee, O Lord, to save and preserve us from the ravages of the heathen federal horde, which would despoil our land and destroy our nation," he said in his concluding prayer, noting the number of men on leave and home from Virginia and northern Georgia on this wintry February Sunday of 1864.

"We pray, O God, that you protect the brave defenders of our country, and give them strength to drive the invaders back, even as they are poised to move toward us, move toward Elam and Mim County."

Joanna pulled her shawl closer around her as William helped her into the wagon for the trip back to the house. "It is snowing harder, Cousin William," Joanna said, smiling down at him as the snow started to fleck and accumulate on his battered hat. "I managed to get the mule hitched up and she cooperated and allowed me to make the trip to town to come to church, but the road home will be slick and muddy as the snow covers it; could you drive me home and take dinner with me today, and bring me news of my husband? It was a joy to see you this morning. You should have written me and told me you were coming home on leave. Were you going to pay me a surprise visit?"

"Well, it's the least I could do for both of you," William replied, smiling back at her in the snowfall. "It's starting to fall harder, and how could I tell John I let you get stuck in the snow alone, and yes, I wanted my visit to be a surprise, but as you can see, it won't be."

William kept the wagon's wheels in the middle of the road, hoping John's old mule, 'Maggie' would keep her footing and not slip as the snowflakes grew thicker and carpeted the road and the trees along side.

Her rose bushes, dormant and gaunt in winter, held the frosty accumulation up to them as they arrived at the house. "My roses look so forlorn, but they will bloom and be red this spring," she said.

"I'm sure they will," William replied, "The roses know how to care for themselves."

"I'll put up the mule and the rig, and then get a hearth fire started," William said. "You best better get inside and I'll hurry to get the house warm."

William came from the barn in the back, leaving the mule chomping on hay he provided and the rig sheltered from the storm. He found the house was warming up, a fire glowing in the hearth, as Joanna set the table for two.

"Confederate women know how to fend for themselves, with their men away in the army, we're not completely helpless, we can build fires," she scolded laughingly as he came inside. "I brought in the last of the ham from the smoke house this

28

morning before church, and I had a good garden last summer, so I put up plenty of vegetables in the cellar. This is the remainder of John's last sow hog, but fortunately I have managed to keep her piglets healthy for future meals."

"A meal fit for officers," William said. "We privates don't see meals like this, thanks to the Yankees and General Braxton Bragg, who seemed bent on starving his own men to death at Chattanooga. We were nearly as starved as the Yankees we were trying to starve down in town. Thank you Joanna, this is wonderful."

"How is John?" Joanna asked. "Why didn't he come home?"

"He is as well as any of us after the retreat," William replied. "He told me he felt it was his duty to stay with the company, with word that the federals are reinforcing and preparing to move south into Georgia. He told me he sends his best, and knows you are doing your best to maintain the house and land and support the Cause. He wanted me to look in on you, and see that you are well."

William finished the last of his ham slice as Joanna glanced out the window and watched the snow, still falling steadily, building up on the oak tree limbs out front. "You look well, Cousin William, you still have your lovely smile, you have lost weight, like every other soldier I see who comes home on leave," Joanna said.

William looked at Joanna. Despite the privations and shortages brought on by the Union blockade and the poor railroad service, made even worse by increasing Yankee cavalry raids, her pale skin, so favored among women of the south, still glowed in the shadow of the oil lamp light, and the light of the fire place. He still admired the heartiness of this woman who did the work expected of her, maintaining the house and land, who could build a fire to ward off the winter cold and probably could have managed to drive a rig home in the snow, but she chose to have him drive her home and William was glad to be with her again.

"Thank you for a wonderful meal and even more wonderful company, Joanna," he said. "This is my next to last day of furlough, have to use the rest of the time to get back to the army so I'm afraid I have to head back. I will tell John I saw you and that you are well."

"It's still snowing William! How are you going to get back to Elam in the snow?" Joanna asked. Her attention was now on him, after looking out the window.

"I guess the same way I get around in the snow and the cold up in Dalton," he replied, smiling. William picked up his wool scarf and the hat he had placed in the chair near the door.

"William", she said. "Catch the morning train back to Dalton. I don't want you to go. May God forgive me, but you came home and John did not...he did not because he does not care, and I know...I know you do, though you will not say it, it is in your eyes, ever since the first day we met when he brought me here from Atlanta and I met you at the station where you greeted us. Oh God, William," she whispered, as she fell into his arms.

He could not resist her embrace, though it was against all he knew, all he believed about honor and trust...that honor and trust he had so struggled to uphold all the days and weeks he spent with her before returning to the war. No, he did not resist. She married a man who did not love her, did not love anyone but himself, but he did love her, had loved her from the first time he ever saw her.

"This is so wrong...so wrong, but John is wrong, not to have come home to you when he could have," William said, holding her, catching her scent, feeling her next to him. "He could have taken leave as I did, in fact I almost begged him to come home with me from Dalton, hoping he would not, but urging him, for fear I could not leave you when I saw you. "God, yes, yes, I have wanted you since the first day I saw you at the station, feeling that John did not deserve you, that selfish fool who knows only how to possess, but not love, but until this moment I was unsure how you really felt about me. I have wished over and over that it was I who had brought you to Elam, that it was I who found you in Atlanta."

The warmth of the hearth fire blended with the warmth of their bodies as they unclothed, she revealing her white round breasts swelling with desire as she saw his bronze toned nakedness. They held each other closely, the bed cover's coolness giving way to their heat.

"William, oh William, do not hold back, give yourself to me," she said, her eyes bright with expectation.

He looked beneath him, her body and hair spread under him, waiting. "Joanna, my Love, you have long been my love, though I dared not express it until now, now you must know, and I shall not deny you."

At the height of their passion they held each other, their moisture blending. She rested her head on his matted chest and she kissed him. "Oh, darling, I could not remove myself in time," he said. "I hope, God I hope, and his voice drifted into silence as she placed her arm around him and drew him so close he felt her heart beating against his.

"My heart, your heart," she said. "Do you hear them, do you feel? You are my heart, I felt you, your hot flowing spring deep inside me, flooding me, awakening me; Oh my love, whatever happens, we have had this glorious moment, this unforgettable moment."

William rose from the bed, still holding her warm hand and went to the washbasin. Here in this blessed place, there was life and love; yes, forbidden, but so far away from the smoke, the hell, the noise, the broken bodies, the oozing bleeding horror of the battle ground, from men who looked like broken, discarded dolls hurled from the sky and dashed against the earth. He moistened his handkerchief he had retrieved from his jacket and placed it softly against her forehead, to sooth her, and Joanna smiled up at him.

"God, I wish this was Eden before the fall, that I was Eve and you were Adam, that this land had never known death or war or suffering. Oh William, the goodness is so fleeting." Joanna looked up at this man who had just taken her to Heaven.

"So fleeting, so rapidly we live and love, then I have to go back but at least not until morning, my love," he replied. "At least not until morning."

Chapter 4

The streetlight outside William's door cast its yellow glow upon Elam, now a snowy ghost land. William hoped the electricity would not fail this time as it had in the last storm, but he knew that ordinarily snow did not burden the tree limbs and cause them to fall and snap power lines. He was glad Bobbie was with him this night; they had not seen much of each other this week and he felt she was safer with him and he wanted the warmth of her company in the warmth of his home.

"You read that so beautifully," Bobbie said, breaking the silence in the room that held them both after William finished reading Joanna's letter. "Sunshine, she called him her sunshine. I long for your touch, your taste and your scent upon me, your precious smile glowing down at me."

"It is so intimate and sweet, what this letter is revealing," William said. "Here we have history's very essence, we're learning how two people felt, how their times were affecting them nearly a century and a half ago, and yet, reading this, it seems like yesterday."

The glow from the hearth lit Bobbie's face, highlighted her cheeks and reflected in her deep brown eyes. She rose from the couch, her jeans brushing against his leg, and looked out the window. "Yep, its winter out there," she said, grinning as she turned back to him. "Looks like I'm snowed in and I'll have to stay for breakfast."

She returned to the couch, caressed his hair, and took his right hand in hers.

"You know I would have come over here, I didn't want to be alone tonight and I didn't want you to be alone, and now, yes, you're right, to find this revelation, these letters that tell us how they really felt, so contrary to what has come down through all these years. Their love was forbidden, William, ours is not and never has been. In this century, this night, I long for your touch, your taste and smell, your precious smile glowing down at me. She touched his lips with her tongue, his fingers found their way to her breasts. The firelight glowed on their nakedness as they soothed and tasted each other.

"Ummmm, slow down, slow down Professor, remember, we're snowed in, and we have all night," she said. "Oh, God, William, darling, darling, give yourself to me, I want to feel you deep inside me....William....William, she cried, and he felt ecstasy as he released in her.

"You are so warm and rich," she said, smiling, the perspiration making her face glow even brighter in the hearth fire light. "My sweet professor, my darling, sweet William," she said. He lay down beside her, and held her tightly.

"Heart beat to heart beat," she said. "I feel your heart, do you feel mine?"

"Heart beat to heart beat," William replied.

Chapter 5

John Carter sat beside the smoldering remains of his campfire and lifted his tin cup, trying to savor the last of the federal coffee from a captured haversack as dawn broke over the cool, wet woods, where he and the rest of what was left of Company 'G' were positioned.

Sullen clouds overhead meant another day of rain and red mud and unseasonable weather for June, as if the sky had set in to punish the men in blue and gray for scarring and tearing the Northwest Georgia landscape and leaving their bodies in its ground.

Shadowy figures approached; tired, wet and grimy in their threadbare jean-cloth jackets and tattered cotton pants. John recognized them as Company 'G' men returning from their picket posts. "Morning John", William Carter said. "They're not doing much, at least not yet, got their pickets out, staying low and quiet...watching us while we watch them."

"Any of that coffee left?" John accepted William's cup, taken from his belt, and shared the remaining warm, dark liquid. William took a sip, laid his Enfield down carefully at half cock and removed the percussion cap with the lock plate facing up, and wearily sagged to the ground, and both men were silent.

William broke the quietness. "Guess you know what's on the other side of the hill behind us

37

yonder," he said. "Who could ever believe...we fought them across Tennessee, drove them out of Georgia last September, nearly starved them in Chattanooga...how did it all get turned around?" he sighed. "And here we are, with them just across the creek where you and me fished, the hill there where we hunted, and less than a mile from your house....damn!"

"How is Joanna?" The question burned and cut the man whose home was just over the hill, whose wife, as far as he knew, was there.

"She has to know by now the fighting is close. Reckon she got out...maybe went down to Elam?" William offered.

John looked up from his cup. "Don't know, I hope so," he said, as he reached inside his jacket and felt Joanna's letter she wrote and sent to William that had fallen out of William's bedroll. "Thanks for loaning me your blanket, made a good pillow."

"Just one less thing I had to tote while on picket," William said. "Guess I'll get it back from you now. Need to try to sleep for a while, but I'm keeping my belt on and my trappins' handy, we may have to get to moving soon."

John watched his cousin tuck his haversack beneath his head for a pillow, pull his dark hat down over his face, and curl up next to the fire. The sun rose higher to reveal the creek and the position of the dismounted federal horsemen, their swallow tailed, candy striped banner visible through the trees. He waited until William was asleep, then moved away under a young pine, the wind made it sigh as he sat beneath it, read the letter, and let her words burn him again.

"So I am cold," he said to the pine tree. "I am cold and you are sunshine, Cousin William, and now Joanna carries your child, a child conceived in deceit, in a lie and now you shall pay for that lie. You will never see that child! You will never have to lie about it or try to make me think I, not you, fathered it. Yes, Cousin William, the only man I thought I could trust...you shall pay."

The Sharps round from a Union carbine chipped a piece of pine bark six inches above John's head and then he heard the firing across the creek grow more frequent, the Yankee rifles barked and banged and puffs of smoke began to appear.

"Form a Line! Form a line! But stay low and under cover!" Company G's first sergeant yelled. John took advantage of the cover and made his way back to the cook fire, where William was looking out, his Enfield capped and ready.

"Here's your rifle, John," William yelled. "Better load it and get ready, looks like they want to move us out of the woods." Federal fire was zipping through the trees now, clipping more bark, kicking up ground.

"Stay low now," the sergeant cautioned. "Don't waste your fire."

Company G's slow but accurate return fire began to bring blue coated cavalrymen down. Two bodies were visible where there was not enough cover and the men were exposed, then an exploding artillery round blew out the top of an old hickory tree, its limbs splintering, crashing to the ground among the men.

"Goddamn, they got cannon!" the sergeant yelled. "They're gonna pin us down with it and then rush us! William and John Carter get over here and bring them Simpson boys with you!"

The four soldiers stumbled over smashed hickory limbs, moving close to the ground toward the sergeant to stay below the fire from the federal line.

"All right, dammit, I want you to move around to the right, cross the creek and find that artillery! They got two full companies in front of us, and we can't hold here with them shells digging into us and pinning us down! Carter, you take your cousin and them twins and get going now, you know what to do...we'll give you what covering fire we can...Now move!"

Another round crashed into Company G's position, this time, lower, this time killing. William looked behind him where the Simpson twins had been following. A split second before...they were there, rifles in hand, hats pulled down, a split second later, they lay in a mangled bloody heap, twitching, moving, but no longer breathing, streaked in red. In a dying gesture, Elijah had reached for his brother James to touch his arm, to let him know he was near...to let him know whatever it is a brother lets his brother know when he is dying with him.

"God," was the only word William could muster. He had seen many men die, many from Company G, too many in this hell he had lived in for two years, but it was the first time he saw two brothers die together. "God," he repeated.

John looked back to see the two boys lying where the cannon ball had exploded. "This is going to be hard on their mother Emma, down in Elam,"

William said, still staring at their bodies. "So close to home, God...God."

"Come on," John said. "Sooner we find that Yankee gun the sooner we can stop it from killing anyone else. Come on, William, you've seen dead men before."

"These are dead boys, John, Goddammit! Dead boys! Boys we knew, boys we saw grow up, dead not five miles from home!"

Another artillery round arched into the woods where they stood, crashing down, making a gaping hole in the underbrush near them.

"And we're less than a mile from my house!" John yelled. "If we don't get moving them Goddamn Yankees are going to keep firing their guns and kill us all! Come on, William!

"John, when we get through this, if we do, got something I need to say to you."

"Well, all right, but no time now!"

From the rate of fire John and William could tell it was just one gun, providing close support for the soldiers preparing their advance across the creek. The noise of the fighting grew fainter as they drew away from it, skipping from tree to tree, crouching...even crawling at times to stay as low as they could and out of sight of the enemy carbines.

John remembered a narrow, shallow spot...a spot where he had crossed the creek many times before, on his way back to his house. John crossed, William followed him, then John hand signaled to stop and stay still. He waved William next to him, and nodded in silence to their front.

Twenty-five yards away three sweating federals, their dark, mud stained shell jackets unbuttoned, served their mountain howitzer as if in a trance of frenzied worship of their squat, short bronze barreled god, causing it to belch its deadly twelve pound balls with smoke and flame, the concussion making it roll back on its wheels.

"They're fast, they're good," William thought as he drew a bead on the number one man, the crewman who primed and fired the gun. John aimed at the loading soldier, the crewman with the rammer who swabbed the barrel to extinguish its hot ambers so the next round could be safely loaded and then shoved it down to the breach when he received it. The third man was moving forward with another round taken from an ammunition box mounted on the back of a mule behind the piece.

It was an easy shot for the two men who had killed with their British made guns at 250 yards into massed formations, and the heads of the two cannoneers burst open, flinging blood and brain matter that spattered and mixed with the mud on their uniforms. The round bearing Yankee, no older than the Simpson twins, stood stock still, frozen in surprise, not comprehending or believing what had just happened.

John already had thrust another round down his rifle barrel, placed the cap, fully cocked it and fired before it occurred to the boy to try to move to safety. He had turned to run just as John's round struck him between the shoulder blades, and he fell, bright red streaming from his mouth...staining the ground.

William and John moved from their brushy concealment and toward the now silent howitzer. The dying boy was still breathing slightly, staring at the sky as John walked toward him.

"Reb," the boy said, "I ain't no harm to you now... could I have a drink of water...please?"

William was looking at the cannon and viewing the remains of the two dead men. "I reckon you can boy, but first, I fancy that pistol you got there," John said, as he reached down and removed the trooper's Colt from its holster. He slid his canteen from his shoulder, held the boy's head up with his arm, and let him drink.

"Thank you, Reb," the round bearer said, "God bless you."

"God bless you," John replied, as he grinned and cocked the pistol, and fired it directly into the boy's face, dissolving it into a shapeless unrecognizable mass, the round hitting him between the eyes. The young Federal's blood splattered John's jacket, and he wiped it as he stood up.

William heard the shot and turned toward him startled. "John, what...why....Ain't we done enough killin' just now to suit you?"

"Not quite enough, William, not quite enough," John replied.

John cocked the pistol again, aimed at William's chest, and fired. The .44 caliber ball found its mark, tearing William's heart into shreds; he was dead before he hit the ground near the fallen Yankee gunners.

John threw the pistol down next to the dead boy's body and walked over to where William lay still.

"Reckon you don't need to say anything to me now, William", he said to his dead cousin's body. "Now you have paid...paid in full, Cousin, and nobody but me is going to know that you did not die gloriously in battle, you died because you cheated and lied."

Chapter 6

Joanna had listened to the thunder on the other side of the ridge from the house, knowing it was not thunder, knowing it was the noise of death made by men killing men. She had placed her hands to her head, hoping to drown it out.

Now there was silence, but the silence was louder, and not knowing what it meant, she wished she had followed William's advice and left for Elam. She did not know war, felt that she could face whatever it brought on her own, but she had heard its sound, knew its breath and touch was near, and she was afraid.

She thought of William and grew restless, rising from her chair by the window, wondering if he was one of those who had seen and felt and made the thunder beyond the ridge.

She walked toward the door, passing the wall mirror, and saw the fear in the face of the woman who glanced back at her. From the road came another sound, faint at first, then louder as they drew closer, a sound of tin touching leather, clinking, clanging, and thudding feet against the earth. She watched the thin, haggard men from the front porch as they moved from the ridge and up the road. They carried their rifles over their right shoulders, it seemed they could take the weight better that way, but still they looked heavy as they trudged past the oaks in the yard.

One of the soldiers, a short grisly corporal, stopped and talked to a tall sergeant as he gestured toward the house and then approached up the walkway. It was John. His dirt and bloodstained jacket hung loose on him and his sweat stained, battered light brown kepi was propped back, revealing a sunburned forehead and a grimy, bearded face.

He placed the Enfield against the banister and removed his blanket role and haversack and laid them on the walkway at the foot of the porch steps.

"Hello Joanna," he said. "I cannot stay long, but I thought you should know, William is dead. You're beloved William is dead, but I am still alive. I hope that does not trouble you too much, darling. I thought perhaps you had left here with the fighting coming so close, and gone to Elam, but since you stayed, you must have heard the shooting and the cannon. William and I stopped that cannon and the company stopped the Yankees from crossing the creek... but now William is killed."

Joanna could only stare out into space, not seeing the road and the field beyond, not seeing the gray sky overhead. She would not cry, not in front of him. Her face expressionless, she could scarcely breathe.

"You have blood on your coat...are you hurt, John, are you wounded?" she asked. "Come sit and rest, let me get you some water. You must tell me how he died."

John walked up the steps and sat down, trailing creek mud onto the porch.

"Ah, it feels good to just sit...but don't bother with the water. I have only a little while before I must rejoin the company, they are already suspicious of Georgians with the army, so many have deserted lately to just go home and get out of the war and be with their families."

"No, my darling, this is the blood of a Yankee I killed, a Yankee helping to load the cannon. William and I shot down the cannon crew. They were firing directly into the company and killing our men. The Simpson boys are among the killed, just about all the boys who died are from Elam and Joanna...William is dead."

"Yes, you told me," she whispered. "Why did you want to tell me again, why did you say, my beloved William?"

"Well, he was your beloved wasn't he darling? You always thought a lot of him and so did I; we were like brothers, more than cousins, only I know now that he meant more to you than he should have," John replied, failing to hide his slight smile, his eyes now attempting to pierce and probe her face, not searching for sorrow, but for guilt.

John reached into his jacket pocket, pulled out William's letter, and handed it to her.

"You see, my love, I read this letter you sent him. It fell out of his blanket roll I was resting on after he loaned it to me before the Yankees started firing at us. I read what you think of him, and I read what you really think of me, and I read what the whoring you did with him has brought you. Elam will hear of how William fell bravely

47

defending Mim County; how a Yankee gunner's pistol killed him, but my dearest, they will never know that while William died from a Yankee's bullet, it was I who fired the gun."

She looked down at the dirty, bloody man sitting in the rocker on her porch, a man she did not love, and now hated. She could stay no longer in the presence of the man who had killed William. She felt her face flushing as she moved silently back into the house.

John was staring out at the road to Elam; he continued speaking, continued smiling, his teeth glinting through the dirty beard. "Yes, my love, you are mine now and your betrayal has brought you to nothing. You will be my dutiful, loving wife in the years to come, if I survive this damn war, which has to be over soon, God knows we can't hold out much longer against Sherman. I will give your child my name, of course, dearest, as far as anyone knows beyond this front porch, it will be mine, conceived when I returned to you after the fight at the creek, and we decided with war and death so close, we wanted to have a child so you would have someone to remember me by if I met my end. But as long as you live, I will never let you forget your treachery...your unfaithfulness to me. That is the way it's going to be, my darling."

The Colt pocket pistol lay in the desk drawer. "Ain't gonna tote a hand gun around when I got an army rifle, just excess baggage, besides pistols are for officers," she recalled John telling her the night before he left to go back to the army. "It is large enough to stop whatever or whoever may bother you, but small enough for your hand", he had told her. "Just don't shoot yourself with it or let anyone take it away from you." Beneath the gun was the letter William had written her after his return to the army in February.

She picked the letter up and caressed it with her eyes and read it again; she had read it over and over since he had left her.

8th of March 1864
Near Dalton with the army

My Blessed Joanna,

I take pen in hand to write you a few lines to let you know that I have returned safely and all is well except we are all cold here in these quarters, but in good spirits.

I sincerely trust you received my image I had made in Atlanta on my way back to Dalton and that it is a decent likeness of me, it appeared to be like it was. The photographer loaned me a coat and cravat as I wanted to look my best for you and decided I would not have it taken in my uniform as so many of the boys do.

The Army is faring better now that we are finally out of the cruel clutches of Braxton Bragg, who the men are convinced is the best Confederate general the Yankees ever had, at least that is the common joke among us here.

We are now under the command of General Joe Johnston, a short but sharp little officer, a Virginian, like General Lee, whose talent matches his turnout, I believe.

He has seen fit to get us more and better rations, and new clothes and shoes, and we hear he has vowed to make Sherman pay for every inch of ground, and defeat him and send him packing at first opportunity.

So the army is better, and now I turn my concern and longing to you, my love.

How sweet was our union, the day and night I spent with you, how close I hold the memory and thought of that sweet time close to me when the night winds howl here, and I stand my sentinel post in the cold dawn.

When I returned John asked of you, but his thoughts are with his corporal stripes and he has become quite the martinet, paying such attention to duty and has expressed hardly a thought of you and your welfare.

We get along as cousins and kinsmen should, and I cannot help feel betrayal of him, but I cannot overcome a feeling that I have never had for a woman after we held each other, became one with our touch, bodies, minds and hearts, and I choose to live with that betrayal and believe God will understand and forgive in the end.

I know John will not understand or forgive either of us, and that is a burden we will have to bear in time; but my longing and wanting and love overcome any thoughts of dread I may harbor.

My only real dread is being separate from you...damn this war and the destruction and death it has caused and will cause before it is over.

But how sweet, how sweet, my dearest, are my thoughts of you, as sweet and pure and lovely as your roses in front of the house that you love so much. We may lose everything, in the end, but we will never lose each other.

I must close now, guard duty beckons. Write soon,

Yours for now and for eternity.

William

"We will never lose each other," she said, quoting the letter's final paragraph. "We will never lose each other."

John had not noticed her absence from the porch. She could hear him talking, the self-satisfied, almost cheerful tone of his voice carried out into the yard, thinking she was still standing behind him, that she was still hearing all his words.

"When I return from the war, Joanna, I will plant closer to the creek, where the bottom land is rich. I will plant cotton dearest; I'll bet you cotton prices will be sky high no matter who wins this damn thing, and we will prosper and you, my

51

darling, will appreciate my generosity and forgiveness for your sin against me and God. And of course, William has already done penance for his sin against me."

The shot from the pistol rang out and blood flowed bright red from the back of John's head. The porch rocker stopped its back and forth movement; he slumped down in it and there was no more talk about his plans for his home and Joanna. John Carter was dead.

Joanna guessed that one more gunshot would not be noticed by anyone, with all the shooting that had taken place this day. She went back into the house and sat and all was quiet. She reached into the desk drawer... removing a pencil and a piece of stationary. William's words came back to her ..."We will never lose each other."

She gathered William's letters including the letter John handed her and placed them into her travel trunk in the bedroom, closing it shut. She had placed the pistol on top of the desk, and went to retrieve it.

Another shot rang out, and then it was silent again at the house beneath the oaks on the road to Elam.

Chapter 7

August 1936

'Ma' Lavonia was dying. Lucille was sad but also relieved that her grandmother's suffering would be ending soon, no more pain, no more coughing, no more moaning in the night, no more haunting recollections of a war that lingered in her memory, a nightmare that would not die; no more longing for a dead sister slain when the shadow of that war crept up on her in her country home miles away from Atlanta.

Lucille walked out on the front porch to see the beginning of another sultry, sticky, smothering August day, the morning sun at 7:30 was already beginning to swell and beam down out of an indifferent copper tainted sky on the houses and homes on Willow Street.

She could hear the morning traffic, the streetcars making their peculiar humming, clunking noise as they took the shop workers and mill workers to their jobs downtown along the steel rails down the center of Bankhead Avenue.

Lavonia wanted her coffee; a hot drink in hot weather which she drank off and on all day when cool water was better for her. The old woman could remember when there was no coffee, not much of anything to eat or drink 72 years ago during the dangerous days of August, 1864 when no one in Atlanta was sure they would make it back if they ventured too far from home. The war destroyed Atlanta and her home on Peachtree

Road. The war had killed Joanna Carter, who went to live with the farmer from Elam, from Mim County, John Carter.

How many times had Lucille heard Lavonia lament Joanna's departure that cold wet autumn day in 1863 with a Confederate fighting for a cause she despised? Lavonia never heard from or about her sister child again until word came that she and John were killed in a Federal Cavalry raid. That is how she thought of Joanna, the 'sister child', born eight years after she was born, the change of life' baby, the final member of the Bohannon Carter household.

Bohannon Carter was a Yankee come south from Ohio, an engineer by trade, who had arrived to help bring steam locomotive transport to North Georgia. Surrounded by a slave and cotton economy, Bohannon kept his non-slave holding beliefs and he and his family suffered the consequences. It was his trade that led to his death north of Marietta on the Western and Atlantic Line in a boiler explosion when Lavonia was 14 and Joanna was only six. The two girls and their mother, Juliet Anne, a North Carolinian by birth, remained in Atlanta. Juliet would not hold a slave and would not have had any use or money for one if she had been so inclined.

She was from the mountains where cotton was not planted and there was little need of slaves. It was all the hill country folk could do to grow their own food crops on land they farmed themselves.

54

Lavonia considered it the Lord's providence that when Juliet went to join Bohannon, when she died of the fever in '56, she was old enough to keep the household, old enough to care for Joanna and earn money as a seamstress, but even as secession fever swept the sprawling railroad city, she kept her mother and father's belief about slavery, and remained a Unionist. She was not alone; there were other Union minded Atlanta citizens, but they kept their sentiments to themselves.

It became a matter of simple survival for Lavonia, she had to care for the 'child sister', give her a home, nurture her, protect her, so much so that she feigned allegiance to these vain, determined Southerners, to make them think she shared their precious cause, and joined in caring for their wounded men in gray and butternut, shipped south from Tennessee and Kentucky battlefields to be cared for. She mended their tattered clothing, rolled their bandages, and assisted the surgeons in treating their grievous wounds.

In this way Lavonia held onto the work that provided the money that sustained her and allowed her to care for her sister who had become more like a troublesome daughter, but instead of showing her now well known talent of altering and making dresses for Atlanta ladies, she was assembling Rebel uniforms, cut by the Confederate tailor in the recently established clothing shop set up under the Army's quartermaster system.

Chapter 8

1864

"I'm going down to the hospital," Joanna announced, after breakfast one morning shortly after news came to Atlanta about the fighting just south of Chattanooga. Many of the wounded from the battle were arriving by train and being taken to the hospitals.

"That so," Lavonia replied, looking up at the 'sister child' a smaller carbon copy of herself, with the slender figure, auburn hair and fair skin they both had inherited from Juliet, and square jaw and wide set flashing green eyes Bohannon had given them. Lavonia enjoyed sewing, seated in the front porch cane rocker, which swept the front of their small wooden white frame house. When Bohannon had it built near the railroad line twenty years earlier just north of Atlanta's circular city limit, the town, which sprang up one mile in each direction from a stake in the ground, was then known as Marthasville.

"You're going to the hospital, to tend to broken, bloody, dirty men, all seventeen years of you, without me going with you, is that right?"

Joanna frowned, "I'm old enough, I know what to do, seen you do it often enough, and I don't care how you really feel about the South and the war, those boys are hurt and need help."

"Is staying here and helping me around this house so much more of a cruel fate that you would

prefer being in a place of suffering and death?",
Lavonia asked.

"The chores will be here when I get back, this
house will be here when I get back, and you, loving
sister, will undoubtedly be here when I get back,
and I'm not going to be gone all day," Joanna said.

"Would not count on that, Girl...Old Doctor
Taylor will put you to work and you won't get back
'til after sundown."

Lavonia loved Joanna's expression of
compassion for the wounded Rebels as much as
she loved her. At the same time, she could not
help but wonder if she saw this as a chance to meet
a man and decided to pester her about it. "Besides,
how do I know you don't just want to meet soldiers
and not tend to them?"

"Lavonia, there are other places in this town to
meet soldiers besides the hospital," Joanna said.
"I want to go to help, not help myself."

Lavonia sighed, and looked up at Joanna,
waving her hand in resignation.

"I don't care what's going on down there, how
badly Doc Taylor says he needs help, you get back
here before supper time, you hear."

"Yes, Sister, I'll let you know the latest news
from town, and I promise, I'll be back for supper"
Joanna said as she tied on her sun bonnet and
went down the walkway that led to the road to
town.

In her 17th year there was not much that
troubled Joanna, other than the war and the fact
that so many of Atlanta's young men had left for

Virginia and Tennessee to fight in it. So many of them her age, or near her age, she had learned, would not be coming back home, would never be seen again by her or anyone else.

But she had really not known most of them, so common was the knowledge in Atlanta that her parents and her sister who was now raising and caring for her were 'Yankee-minded', that their sentiments were not with the south, Atlanta, or its people, so she found herself shunned, and it made her unhappy.

"Well, I'm not Yankee-minded," Joanna thought to herself. *"If I was, would I be on my way to the hospital to help out, to do what I can to care for these boys?"*

She knew that Lavonia had visited the hospital to help in the interest of keeping her customers, to demonstrate to them that she would do what she could even if she did not agree with why they were sending their men away, only to see them return torn and shattered. They both had seen and tended to the human damage of war and battle, the bleeding, the suffering, the moaning, crying and dying; Joanna was going there because she cared, really cared, and now she was going again, on this sunny early autumn day, too pretty for pain and death.

Peachtree Road was hard packed and easy to walk on until Joanna was close to Five Points. There it turned into a red, sloppy morass, stirred and broken by mules and wagons hauling army equipment, supplies, and by the ambulances carrying the wounded coming in from the trains. Atlanta was a jumble, a confusion of people back burdened with all their possessions, rolled up in hand sown quilts of many earthen colors, slipping, stumbling, trying not to mire down in the smelly red goo that kept trying to snare them and trap them. They had come to Atlanta to avoid living behind federal lines. They had come from mountain valley cabins and hillside farms and Joanna wondered if they would not have been better off if they had just stayed home and took their chances with the

"Where are they all going, and what will they find when they get there?" Joanna wondered. *"They certainly will have a hard time finding a place in this town."*

The refugees added to Atlanta's crowding, already created by the army and its traffic and its wounded; so many wounded from the fighting on the banks of that creek they called Chickamauga. Joanna had read that was its Indian name for 'River of Death'. Students at Atlanta Medical College no longer learned in class, they could get practical instruction by treating the soldiers' wounds. It was overflowing with battle injury and the sickness that followed and by the many diseases that plagued the army even when its men were not fighting.

The hotels hardly had any room for lodgers. They were too full of those who were struggling for life. Even the new hospital they had built at the Fair Grounds had begun to fill up with the war injured, so it was not hard for Joanna to find a place to help.

Just then a swaying ambulance full of bleeding, moaning men splashed red mud on Joanna's blue print dress as she stood in front of the Intelligencer newspaper office. The driver did not notice as he urged his mule drawn cargo of pain to the nearest hospital, so Joanna knew it would do no good to cry out in protest. She decided to just follow the ambulance until it stopped in front of the Excelsior, which once greeted weary out of town railroad passengers, but now housed the hurting from the Army of Tennessee.

As Joanna approached the front doors, she was greeted with the cry of 'Next', as the surgeons called for another soldier to be placed on their bloody tables. Amputations of legs and arms had become more efficient, taking only 15 to 20 minutes on the average. Amputation was the only treatment known to save a man's life after the bullet shattered the bone, but Joanna knew from previous visits the surgery was always followed by shrieks of pain, and then silence from shock and resignation with knowledge that the amputee was forever maimed.

If there was one thing John Carter was sick of it was the sight of blood and the wounded and the hospitals. He was sick and tired of being a hospital steward. He knew it kept him away from bullets and death, which he feared, but not the smell and the sight of the dying and dead, which he hated.

Still, *'better thee than me'* was the motto that kept him going these days.

Better thee than me'...that thought kept him alive at Chickamauga. After the first day up there he got out of the fighting and got himself a field hospital job behind the lines. He got out after a federal shell clipped a tree branch over his head and it landed right on him, knocking him down. That tree branch turned out to cause an arm wound good enough to get him off the field but not really bad enough to hurt him much at all.

"Call me a hospital rat if they want to," he said to himself. *"Them that accused me of being a rat are dead and laying in a burial pit in them woods up there, and I'm still alive. Course working in this hell-hole here in Atlanta is a poor excuse for living...God I hate this damn place."*

"Carter, there's another load of wounded comin' in, get crackin'" the surgeon closest to him called out. "And put this volunteer girl to work, she just got here and we need all the help we can get today."

"Well, you're certainly the best thing I've looked at in this place all day," John said to Joanna, "even if you did fall in the mud."

Joanna smiled at this short, soiled soldier, grinning at her from the midst of the bedlam in the hotel lobby. "Are all these soldiers from the fighting at Chickamauga? I heard the battle was terrible but we won, and there are so many wounded."

"There were many wounded, very many," John replied to the fair skinned, green-eyed girl in the muddy print dress holding his attention. "I narrowly escaped with my life, got wounded the first day, so they sent me here to help tend to them that was hurt worse than me. Yeah, it was a victory, first we've had under Bragg, but one more like this one will use up this army."

"What possessed you to come down to this hell hole on such a pretty day? You ought to be home, tending to your garden or sewing, or something."

Joanna's smile turned to a frown. "Do you doubt my purpose for being here, sir? I only came to help, to see what I could do for these poor boys."

John saw her displeasure and decided to guard his words; he did not want to be unfriendly to the only thing he had seen worth looking at since he had arrived in Atlanta. "Now, Missy, I didn't mean nothin; just funnin' a bit. I think it's a noble thing, you bein' here to help, God knows we need all the help we can get right now, there's so many and we have so few to care for them all."

"Carter, come quick and bring that girl," we've got an amputation to do or this boy is going to die," the surgeon said. A makeshift table made from a hotel room door resting on two wooden barrels was already bloody when the stretcher-bearers placed the young Tennessee cavalryman on it. His blue eyes were wild with pain, the reason he was brought in, obvious for all to see; his right leg, shattered by a federal minie ball. Joanna placed a damp cloth on his forehead, attempting to sooth and cool him.

"You won't let them take it, will ya, Miss...Oh God, please no...I'll never ride again if they take my leg...please, no."

"They got to, Trooper, or you'll die," John told him. "Try to rest easy."

"We're out of chloroform, used it all up already and there is no more, I'm sorry Boy," the surgeon said, looking away, unable to look him in the face. "You'll have to hold on, God willing you can make it."

At that, John's shoulders slumped and he turned to Joanna and saw her wince. The medical man was smeared with blood from the neck down, his apron stained a deep crimson. He picked up his saw and turned to John and Joanna. "Get ready, and God get us through this."

Joanna was not ready for this. When she visited the hospitals it was always with Lavonia, who had shielded her from the worst sights of the suffering. She assisted Lavonia who in turn helped where she could; they had often come to deliver bandages, read to the wounded men, trying to cheer them and get their minds off the hurting, but this was her first real view of a man about to lose a limb.

She heard the first sound of the saw severing bone, and the beginning of the soldier's screams, and she could recall no more. She awoke on a battered couch pushed into a corner of the hotel lobby. John was standing over her.

"Hi, Girl," he said when he saw her open her eyes. "The boy didn't make it...died of shock. A lot of them do that, 'specially when they can't put them under. How do you feel?"

Joanna slowly sat up and looked around at the mayhem that still surrounded her. "What happened to me?"

"You fainted dead away, had to get another soldier to help out, for what good it did that boy, but don't feel bad about it, amputations are hard for anybody to take."

As the late afternoon sun filtered through the windows and the hotel's front door, she saw the spots of blood that had spattered the front of her dress, she was called to help so quickly she did not have time to put on an apron, and she began to cry.

"Oh, God, I've got to get out of here," she sobbed. "It's time to go back home, but not just that, I've got to get out of here, God, this horrible place, this horrible war that kills and maims."

Another steward brought in a wooden bucket with fresh water; John took his tin cup from his belt and dipped it full. "You still look a little wobbly to me, drink this and sit still for a little while. Then I want to see you home and make sure you get back safe. You could get run over with all them wagons up and down the street."

Chapter 9

"She may be 17 now, but I've a mind to take a switch to her when she gets back," Lavonia said aloud as she looked down the rain soaked red clay road to Atlanta. It was past dusk and the sky was gray and had let loose with a cold soaking rain.

"That girl is going to catch her death and I don't need the burden of nursing a sick one right now," she said aloud again, her worry growing with the growing darkness now enveloping the house. She looked down the road from the porch again and made out two shadowy figures coming up through the wet gloom.

"Good Lord, she's brought a Rebel home with her," Lavonia exclaimed, seeing the short corporal who walked beside her sister.

"Hello, Sister," Joanna said. This is John, John Carter from Elam in Mim County. He's fetched me home from the hospital."

"How do you do", John said, removing his battered gray brown kepi. "Miss Joanna here...well, things was a little rough down at the Excelsior which we have turned into a hospital, what with all the wounded and the hurting and all, and with it getting dark, I decided to walk her home. I hope you do not mind."

Lavonia looked at this soiled Confederate, feeling both disdain and gratitude. *"He looks healthy and whole enough, why isn't he at the front instead of Atlanta,"* she wondered. "Well, Mr. Carter, it was very kind and considerate of you to see my sister home. I'm afraid she does not always use good judgment, so I am glad you were kind enough to bring her back where she belongs. Supper is still on the stove and since the hour is growing late, may I invite you to join us?"

"A home cooked meal is mighty hard to turn down, Ms. Carter, and by the way, may I say it is a very pleasant coincidence that we share the same last name. I'm afraid I got to return to the hospital, I was told to get back as soon as I finished escorting Miss Joanna home. I would like to return and take supper with you and Miss Joanna at a more convenient time for everyone, if that is alright."

"You are welcome to do so, sir, more than welcome, perhaps you can tell us about Elam, your home," Lavonia replied.

"I'll take my leave now," John said, "Good night to you both."

The hospital soldier turned and disappeared into the rainy night and Lavonia wasted no time beginning her questions.

"Where did you find that one, girl," she said. "A Rebel! You brought a REBEL back with you, knowing how I feel...and a dirty one at that!"

Joanna could not conceal her impish smirk. "God, Lavonia if you think he's dirty you should see the other ones down in town. Most all of them are dirty and tired, the ones who are not shot to pieces and dying, Atlanta's full of them. Now, you need to give him credit. He saw me home didn't he...he behaved good, didn't he...and tried to be a gentleman."

"At least you could have found an officer to escort you home," Lavonia retorted. "You're fresh and young and pretty, even if you don't have a brain in your head, and to him you must have been a breath of fresh air down there."

"I think I like that little hospital corporal," Joanna replied defiantly. I hope I do see him again, and I hope he does come back for supper."

Joanna stood before her sister, red mud and blood smeared her print dress, water dripped from its skirts and puddled on the front porch floor. There was complete darkness now and it masked the road and the front yard in shadows.

In the days ahead Lavonia planned to keep her sister close, no more walks to Atlanta. There was plenty she could do around the house. Lavonia would remind her of how much she loved the roses that surrounded their home, how they needed tending, how it was her duty to keep them alive and well because they were planted by their mother, and because their father loved them so...she would remind her, and hope.

"Well, get inside and change out of those muddy clothes before you catch your death, supper is getting cold," she told Sister Child.

Chapter 10

Through September into October, Atlanta drowned in Army of Tennessee wounded. Hospitals all the way south to Griffin, even to Macon were also filled with the injured and the sick, and John Carter grew even more sick and weary of his hospital steward duties, so much so he welcomed news that soon he would be called back to the army and Company 'G'. Finally the stream of casualties from Chickamauga began to diminish, a full month and a half after the fighting.

For civilians and soldiers of the South alike, Chickamauga was a breath of hope, that hope so crushed in July at that Southern Pennsylvania crossroads called Gettysburg. So John was getting his wish. First though, he wanted leave. He wanted to go see about his holdings near Elam, the house and the farm he had left behind in the hands of his town cousins, who he neither liked nor trusted. He also had no word on how Company 'G' had fared since the battle, especially his cousin William, the only one of the town Carters he had any use for. And, John wanted something else. He wanted Joanna Carter about as badly as he wanted anything, as badly as that sister of hers intended to deny her to him.

His attempt to see her again a week after he had escorted Joanna home had not gone well. On a day pass he had walked out to the house to find Joanna and Lavonia not at home. Today was the

71

first chance he had to try again, and he saw Joanna busy with the roses that lined the front of the place. He had no way of letting them know he was coming, and had hoped his appearance would not be an unwelcome surprise. It was not to Joanna, it was to Lavonia.

John was not a lover of roses, but he had to admit these roses were about the loveliest he had ever seen. They almost appeared mystical...a backdrop of blooming color at a place so close to the scars of war Chickamauga had created and sent to Atlanta.

"Hi there, Joanna, you sure have a green thumb", he said, knowing his words would possibly startle her as he spoke before she saw him, she was pre-occupied.

She was startled, but not displeased and put down her trowel. She brushed off the yard dust as she stood before him.

"How have you been, what have you been doing?" she asked, noticing that John had at least attempted to clean his faded shell jacket and his trousers and wore what appeared to be a clean shirt.

"Ah, the wounded kept pouring in from Chickamauga, so we've been busy with that, but looks like that's beginning to slack up, so I finally got the time to come back out. Don't know much 'bout growing things, but your roses are sure pretty", he replied. "So how have you been? Have not seen you back in Atlanta."

Joanna looked down at her faded housedress, a plain brown creation of Lavonia's, which she never wore away from home. "I'm sorry you had to see me like this, all stained from working in the dirt."

"I'm just glad to see you, Joanna, your gardening dress don't bother me none," John said. "I admire a woman who knows how to work and get things done around the place, not like them high and mighty gals in their hoop skirts back in town who don't know how to do a thing except primp up and put on airs."

Joanna smiled, and with that smile John knew this was the woman he wanted with him on his lands in Mim County, the woman who would obey him in time and who he could teach to manage things instead of his Elam cousins. She was a bit simple, but strong, strong and becoming enough as far as he was concerned to give him the pleasure and satisfaction he craved and desired, maybe even give him a boy child who would carry on his name.

He straightened his stance, stood squarely on his feet, and looked into her eyes. He had never made a proposal, never knew a woman he wanted to propose to until now.

"Joanna, it's time I talked to your sister. The army is calling me back, Bragg is trying to lay his hands on every man he can now that he has the Yankees hemmed up in Chattanooga, but I want to go back to Mim County first and I want you to go with me. Joanna, I want you for my wife, to share my home, my land, my life. I want someone to come back to when this damn war is over, if I live through it."

Joanna was not expecting all this all at once from her 'little hospital corporal', although, as she had told Lavonia, she was fond of him despite her objections. All at once, her desire for change in her life, her longing to start her own life away from Atlanta and her sister who acted more like a stern mother, came to a point. Here was this man from Elam offering about as big a change as she could imagine.

"*Yes, yes, yes,*" she thought. *Here is my chance, my chance to begin something for myself, and here is the man who will give it to me, and I can learn to love him, I love him already for wanting me.*

Her voice quavered, her lips trembled as his words electrified her and left her breathless. "Well, go up to the porch and sit in the rocker. I'll go fetch Sister."

John's arrival had not escaped Lavonia's attention, nor had the conversation that had just taken place, as she watched from the window and saw his approach. As she watched Joanna coming to the front door, it was with a sense of dread mixed with sadness, mixed with anger and resentment.

"Well, what does he want?" she asked, as Joanna burst into the house, her face flushed.

"Come see, come listen, don't say or do anything that will make me hate you," Joanna replied.

Lavonia stepped out of the house at her little sister's urging to confront this man who intended to take her away, this man she did not like or trust, this man in Rebel uniform who represented everything she was against.

"Well, Mr. Carter, Joanna tells me you have something you want to talk about. Just what would that be?"

Lavonia knew what it was already, she could tell by Joanna's expression and her excitement. She chose not to sit; she wanted to look down at the short Confederate. John did not like looking up at someone, especially a woman, but he put his discomfort aside. After all, he had some big words to say.

"Miz Lavonia, as you know I have not known Joanna very long, in this war people who do not know each other for very long, I believe, can still find genuine feelings for each other, as I have for Joanna. I feel she is a fine, strong woman, the kind of woman I need with me in Mim County to make my place a home. She is a woman I feel I can provide for without reservation, and a woman I want to share my life with. I know I'm a bit older than she is, but not by much, and I have good prospects and a good piece of land and the desire to be successful regardless of how this war turns out."

John felt he had put it together about as well as he could have, considering he was talking to a woman who he knew did not care for him about her sister who he wanted to take away from her.

"Well, I'll give you this, you are matter of fact, but you are talking about Joanna like she is a property acquisition, not a wife, not the woman you love," Lavonia replied. "Do you love her, Mr. Carter?"

John promised himself he would not get impatient if this turned into an inquisition, but he was getting a bit impatient nonetheless. After all, Joanna was of age, it was really up to her.

"Reckon I do, else I would not be sitting here on your front porch telling you I want her in my life, to share my life and my lands and my home. Miz Lavonia, I just wanted to honor you as her sister and only living kin by letting you know my intentions and feelings. Why don't you ask her how she feels?"

Lavonia turned to Sister Child, who had been taking in every word.

"It's time I left here, Sister, to start my own life, and I want to be with him, and go to Mim County. I love you Lavonia, but I want to go."

There was a will in Joanna's face that Lavonia could not dismiss or ignore, and she looked down at the porch floor with resignation.

"I love you too, girl, enough so that I won't stand in the way, but I wish I felt better about this and about this man and about you leaving. You are so young yet, never been away from home, from me, from this place, but you're like your Momma when it comes to knowing your own mind and heart, but I do insist on this; you will marry here at this house. At least grant me that."

"That's fine, Miz Lavonia, but it's got to be soon", John said. "I hear the army will be calling me back and I want time to take Joanna to Mim County."

"How about next Saturday?" Joanna chimed in, excitedly. "I know it's not much time, but with the war and so much happening so quickly...oh Lavonia, the sooner the better!"

"The sooner the better", Lavonia thought, again with sadness and resignation..."*the sooner the better, for you to end one chapter of your life and start a new one, an uncertain one, maybe a disastrous and fearful one full of sorrow with this man you do not know.*"

Dreams were coming true rapidly for Joanna and John, and John knew he would have to act quickly. Joanna said she would get busy getting the house ready for the first and only wedding ceremony it would ever see, John said he would take on the responsibility of finding a minister for the ceremony, since the only pastor Lavonia and Joanna knew was now a chaplain with the army in Virginia. John decided he would call on the Reverend Obadiah Phelps, a Methodist pastor he had seen often at the hospital set up in the Excelsior. He also wrote his cousin William, to tell him he was getting married, and he was coming back to Mim County.

Pastor Phelps has said final words over enough dead and dying men, John thought, maybe he'll be glad to hold a service for a man starting his married life. An obliging man, the Reverend

Phelps agreed to ride John out to Joanna and Lavonia's house the morning of the wedding and drive them both back to Atlanta, where they would stay the night before departing on the train for Elam the next day.

"I am glad to witness what I hope will be a blessed beginning, instead of a sorrowful, woeful ending, as you know I have presided over so many these past weeks," the Reverend told John. "This is happening so quickly, but then so much has happened quickly among our young men and women these days. I trust you have thought this major change in your lives through and are confident and satisfied with it."

"Oh, not to worry there," John replied. The morning was cool and cloudy and light rain pelted the carriage top as they rode toward the house. "We're both ready and wanting this."

A cheery hearth fire greeted John and the pastor as they entered the front room, which was aglow with candlelight. Joanna had decorated the room with her roses.

Lavonia had made up her mind she wanted this to be a happy day for Joanna and was doing her best to conceal her misgivings. She was gracious to the Reverend, and managed to be polite to John. She too had met the pastor on her trips to assist in tending the wounded in Atlanta.

"Reverend, how nice to see you again sir," Lavonia said as she smiled at the clergyman dressed in his black broadcloth coat and vest. "I am so glad you are officiating a happy occasion this time, not a sad one. You may put your horse and rig in the barn out back of the house, need to get it out of this wet."

"Mr. Carter, I must say you look dashing today in your jacket with the buttons shining and gleaming, and you are wearing new trousers, it appears, how impressive!"

His wedding uniform was the result of lucky foraging; its original owner was a wealthy South Carolinian who died of his Chickamauga wounds at the Excelsior. John managed to get the battle and blood stains washed from it and he felt it was quite presentable, certainly better than his old jean wool shell jacket and patched depot issue pants.

Lavonia could not bring herself to call John by his first name. He would be 'Mr. Carter' from now on to her, as a way of showing the distance she wanted from him. The center of attraction this day, Joanna, had not appeared yet, but when she did, she did her best to look radiant, and she succeeded.

She was wearing Lavonia's blue-sprigged muslin dress. Lavonia had added lace to the collar left over from filling a customer's order. The dress did not require much hemming, the sisters were about the same size and height, and it had the desired effect on all present.

"How lovely this bride is," Reverend Phelps exclaimed, "How lovely!"

The approval Joanna really hoped for came from John. "You make me proud and glad to be here today," he said and Joanna beamed with delight.

"You are as fine a bride as any in Atlanta or anywhere else," Lavonia told her, smiling. "I am glad you are happy."

The Reverend cleared his throat, Bible in hand. "We are all assembled. Is everyone ready? Then let us proceed."

The rain was falling harder on the roof, but the hearth fire and the candle light, illuminating the red of Joanna's roses gave the room the modest but cheery warmth and charm Joanna had hoped for as she and John exchanged their vows. Lavonia had prepared a roast chicken with the trimmings for the wedding meal.

"Doesn't look like this rain is going to let up any time soon," John said after everyone had eaten. "Hate to travel in it, but I expect we may as well head back to town. The Excelsior is back to being a hotel again now that most of the wounded have been evacuated out, so we have a room waiting for us, I reserved it yesterday. You about ready, Reverend?"

"Yes, sir, quick as I get the rig out of the barn," he replied.

With the horse and carriage pulled up to the front of the house, it was time for Lavonia to say goodbye.

"Try to stay dry, don't want you to catch cold on your wedding night," she said, trying to smile. "God bless you girl."

"I'll take care of your Sis, Miz Lavonia," John said. "After we get settled, you can come and visit."

"I'll write you Lavonia, I'll write and tell you of life in Mim County, of the farm, of my life with John," Joanna promised.

They got into the carriage, the Reverend urged his horse forward, and within moments they disappeared into the rain and down Peachtree Road. Lavonia, now standing alone, issued a silent prayer that Joanna would keep her promise and write soon.

She would never hear from Sister Child again. She would survive the fighting around Atlanta a year later, and the siege and surrender. She would meet and marry an Ohio Union soldier who came with Sherman, a man named Carter, by coincidence a cousin of her father. They would have a son and a daughter, she would have a life and a home and family, but her children and their children would never know Joanna, and through it all, she would never lose thought or longing for her.

Chapter 11

Joanna thought she had seen a dream, felt a dream coming true with the hospital soldier, only to realize shortly after she left her home on Peachtree Road to be with him, her dream was not coming true.

She had her own notions about what life with a man should be. A man should be gentle, tender, loving, kind, a man as a partner should share his dreams and cares. John Carter, she quickly learned, was none of those things. She was bound to him. After all, she had spoken the vows, and now the words, 'for better or worse' hung heavily upon her.

She began learning about John the first night with him at the Excelsior. The Excelsior was no longer the quaint, comfortable railroad hotel it once had been before the mark of war had changed the face of Atlanta. The lobby, the rooms, the very atmosphere still made it feel like a place of suffering and death.

"Well, Girlie, here we are," John said after he closed the door on their bare, stripped down room, a telling grin on his face, the grin of a man whose long wait for a delicious meal was finally over.

Joanna saw the grin and did not like it. "I am Mrs. John Carter, Mr. Carter, and I am not your 'Girlie'. If you want a 'Girlie', I'm sure you can find one out on the street down on the corner. If you want a wife, I am here, so make up your mind!"

John could see being married to Joanna Carter was going to be a bit more complicated than he expected and he would have to take a different approach to get what he wanted out of her.

"Meant no disrespect," John said. "Guess that's my way of trying to warm up to you, showing you I care. I know who you are and what you are."

"Good," Joanna replied. "You will now escort me to the Excelsior dining room where we will have our first supper together."

"Yes, Mrs. Carter," John replied.

He decided he would bide his time, at least this girl had spunk and a bit of gumption, qualities she would need in the weeks and months to come at the farm east of Elam, but he was still a man weary of waiting for a delicious, sensual meal, and Joanna was on the menu.

The evening meal in the Excelsior dining room was about as good as one could expect for a hotel just emerging from impressed service as a soldier's hospital; chicken and dumplings, more dumplings than chicken, but at least there was plenty of it, and the after dinner coffee was passable. Dessert was too much to hope for, but, in honor of the newlyweds, the waiter managed to come up with apple pie.

"It's good to have newlywed folks at the hotel again," he said, as he brought the pie with the coffee.

John nodded his head in approval, Joanna gave him a big smile, and he smiled back with his broad, black face, beaming down from his tall frame clad in a faded black waistcoat.

"Well, Mr. Carter, if we are to catch the early morning train to Elam, we must turn in early," Joanna said when they returned to their room.

"Don't you think something needs to happen between the time we turn in and when we fall asleep?" John asked. "You asked for our first dinner together, now it's time to spend our first night together."

"I am your wife, sir, not your whore, so don't treat me like one, "Joanna replied. She knew this moment was coming, and now that it was here, she was uncertain how to deal with it; she chose hesitation, laced with fear.

"You don't know yet how to be either, and I think it's time to learn," John said. "And stop calling me Mr. Carter. I am John Carter your husband, and you are Joanna Carter my wife. So go ahead and get ready for bed, and get ready to be with me in it for the first time."

"It is my first time," she said. "Be gentle. Can you be gentle...can you be loving?"

"Like I said," John replied, "It's time for you to learn."

Joanna did not sense love from this man and decided to get through this night and all the nights to come with him the best way she could. She had promised herself she would learn to love him, now she was not sure at all that would ever be.

The train trip to Elam was gray and cold, the sun refusing to allow its rays to warm and illuminate North Georgia's hilly landscape. The trees were alive with the foliage of fall. The wood fueled W & A locomotive chugged and steamed through the trees laden with bright yellow and red color. It would have been a picturesque ride but the glum overcast dulled the scenery, and Joanna sat silently in her seat, silently in her pain, pain she had never experienced before after her first night with a husband who had not been gentle, had not been caring, who only cared about satisfying himself.

John was not silent, continuously chatting about his farm and about Mim County and his plans. He was in a fine mood following his first night with his new wife, his new help mate, as he was calling her. "You have a great deal to look forward to you know, you did good partnering up with me, you will not regret it, you're headed to a good life in Mim County, so cheer up," the cheerful John said.

Joanna turned her head to the window and stared out at the landscape passing by, trying to muster all the determination and endurance her parents and her sister had passed on to her. She envisioned her future in Mim County as John Carter's 'partner', not wife, not his beloved, but his 'partner' and already had reason to know that partner to him meant pleasing him by doing what he expected of her. She asked herself, *"Why didn't I see what he was really like, he was so different when I first met him, he seemed to care about me. Why didn't I listen to Lavonia...why, why?"*

"I know why you're sittin' there so quiet," John said, interrupting her thoughts. "You've had a lot happen to you these past couple of days and I know it's a lot to take in, but you'll get to feeling better once you see the place, and William will be around for a while to help you get used to things."

"William, who is William, she asked. Is he your slave, your hired man, or what?"

John chuckled. "Naw...and I reckon I should have told you before now. William's my town cousin from Elam, the only one of the bunch of relations from town I really have any use for. We joined the Company last year, we was at Chickamauga together and he got wounded a lot worse than me, nearly lost his leg from a shell fragment. Well, he got lucky, they saved the leg and he got sent home so while he's on the mend he said he'll mind the place for me. I wrote him about you; he wrote back, said he's looking forward to meeting you and he'll meet us at the Station."

Joanna wondered if William was anything like John as she tried to picture him in her mind.

Chapter 12

William Carter was of course thankful that the surgeons at Chickamauga had spared his leg, had decided that the bone was not splintered and that they did not need to amputate to save his life, but here in this gloomy morning cold at Elam station the leg was aching, as it always did in such weather. He suspected it was something he would be cursed with the rest of his days, but a cold weather ache and a slight limp was far better than an empty trouser leg.

The wound had not permanently separated him from the army or the war, but it at least had earned him a reprieve, a chance to be home, a chance to be near the hills and the fields and the creek east of Elam at Cousin John's farm.

He was one of the few people who liked John, and he was not sure why. He could be so disagreeable and self-centered most of the time, but still, there was a bond, perhaps formed when John befriended him when he was small, and because John was the one person responsible for him even being alive. It was John who had saved him from drowning when he slipped from the creek bank and fell into the creek near the house on Elam Road, and afterwards had thrown him back into the water and yelled at him to work his arms and legs to keep himself above the water if he did not want to start drowning again. William chuckled to himself as he recalled the memory, his recollection interrupted by the sound of the train steaming and pulling into the station.

"So old John has got himself married," William said out loud to himself, watching the locomotive brake and pull up to the boarding platform. *"Was beginning to wonder if any woman would have the rascal, but there is someone for everyone, I reckon. Wonder what she looks like?"*

She looked pale to William in the morning grayness as she stepped out of the passenger coach, John waving at him as he stepped off behind her. William's first look at Joanna Carter revealed her piercing green eyes set in an oval face with a set, determined jaw.

"Well, you look spry enough cousin," John said as he walked up. "You look like you're healin' up. Want you to meet Joanna, now known as Mrs. John Carter."

Joanna looked at this injured soldier, this brown haired, blue-eyed man, standing before her, smiling at her. *"No, he is not like my husband, not like his cousin, it does not seem to be,"* she thought as she smiled back at him.

"I'm pleased to meet you Joanna," he said, looking into the green eyes, watching her lips smile at him, watching the oval face brighten with the smile. *"She is young, so fresh, so innocent looking; how the hell did John Carter get her into his life,"* he wondered to himself.

"Come on John, let's get this new bride of yours out to her new home on Elam Road and out of this cool damp chill soon as we can," William said.

"Reckon we can get caught up on each other's news on the way out."

"Sounds good to me, let's get going," John replied. "Don't care to tarry around in town any longer than I have to, less you think we need to go over to the store and get some supplies."

"Nope, no need," William said. "After I got your letter I went out and made sure everything's stocked up, so we can just head on out."

For the first time since she had left Atlanta, had left Lavonia, had left everything she knew and had grown up with at the house on Peachtree Road, Joanna was feeling better, she thought that maybe her future was not as dire as she was beginning to imagine it, and this young man, this cousin of John's, was beginning to make the difference.

William was at the reigns of John's wagon pulled by his aging mule, Maggie. John sat beside him, and she sat beside John as the wagon made its way out of Elam and out on the road. Elam was a far cry from Atlanta. It was, like Atlanta, a railroad town, springing up from North Georgia's upper Piedmont on the fringe of the state's hill country when the Western and Atlantic's rails were laid 30 years ago. Joanna counted three churches; a Methodist, a Baptist and a Presbyterian. There was one general merchandise store, a town hall, and a scattering of small shops that catered to Mim County's farming community lining the main street from Elam Depot.

Elam had no hotels. There was one house that appeared to double as a boarding house and a restaurant and at the center of the place, the Mim County Court house, a brick structure with a broad porch that wrapped itself around the building. Across the street was the sheriff's office and jail, and trailing down the street from that were three law offices and one bank, and that was about all there was to the place. Elam was laid out in the form of a square and surrounding the heart of the town were the homes, nothing elaborate, just common looking wood framed white houses with porches and swings that reminded her of the home she left.

Mim County was only slowly evolving from its frontier state when the Cherokee lived on the land. Once out of town the country remained heavily forested, broken only here and there by a farmhouse and cleared acreage planted in row crops, but Joanna noticed, not cotton. *"The South is hungry,"* she thought. *"The soldiers, everyone, is hungry; can't eat cotton."*

John also noticed the crops and turned to William. "What they been plantin' on the land since I've been gone," he asked.

"They've been planting row crops John," William said. "Corn mostly, corn is almost as good a crop as cotton for the price, what with the demand at the market and prices sky high for everything now. Hell, takes a wheel barrel full of money just to buy a sack of meal now. Better plan on keeping planting corn, John, now and after this damn thing is over."

"Pity you got to go back, pity I got to go back to this damn war, even if it looks like we've got the upper hand at Chattanooga right now."

"I know you got to go back to Company 'G' soon, when are you leaving?"

"Well, want to get Joanna settled in, and look over the place, then I reckon I'll be catching the train north day after tomorrow," John replied. "How soon you got to go back?"

"I'm about healed up good enough to report back too," William said. "Was hoping they'd just write me off and I could stay home, but Bragg needs every man, I'm told, so I reckon I'll be seeing you by the end of the month. Maybe if old Bragg don't muck things up, the war will turn our way, we can chase the Yanks out, and who knows, maybe we can all come home to stay."

"Yeah, that would be nice, right enough," John said "but the Yanks won't quit I'm afraid, so I just don't know. It's got to end some day, at some point, just hope we'll live to see it."

As the rig moved slowly toward its destination, her new home, Joanna watched the two men, and listened. They were so similar in appearance, you could look at them and tell they were related, more like an older and younger brother than cousins, both of slight stature, both with blue eyes and almost the same hair color, their voices even sounded alike, and yet, so different. William by his nature, had cheered her and made her hope, John, by his nature, had not. She hoped she would learn that the man she had just met was more like what she envisioned a man should be, for the man she had married was not that vision, but she still held out hope that in time he could be, with time, he could be.

"I will plant roses," Joanna said aloud, the morning John caught the train that would take him back to the army and the war. "This may be John Carter's house, his land, but they will be my roses and I will plant them all across the front of the porch, they will be bright red, they will shine and glow in the sun, and they will be mine, my mark on this place."

Joanna, more than ever now, felt more like a possession than a person, just a convenient addition to the house and farm east of Elam. When she arrived there from the station John wasted no time in making sure she understood her 'place' in his world and on his land, and the night before he left she was reminded of how dominating and selfish he was, and how little he seemed to care or want to share with her.

Joanna just gave him what he wanted, and what he wanted was to be satisfied without any thought of whether she was or not. When he was finished he rolled over, turned his back to her, went to sleep and began snoring, which kept her awake. She had performed her 'wifely duty', but that is how she thought of it, a duty, something you had to do because of a promise, and nothing more.

There was no affectionate farewell, the morning he left for Elam and the train station, just "Goodbye and take care of things, William's gonna help out before he has to leave, I'll write when I get the chance," is all he said when he and William got on the wagon and headed back down the road for town, leaving her alone in the morning chill.

"William," she called out. "Don't forget the roses." He turned and waved his hand as the wagon pulled away.

"I won't," he replied.

The Western and Atlantic locomotive was building a head of steam when they arrived at Elam Station, preparing for its journey north toward the Confederate lines and the ridge line around Chattanooga where Bragg's army held the federal Army of the Cumberland captive after its defeat at Chickamauga.

"Well, say hello to the boys for me," William said, as John got off the wagon, wearing the refurbished uniform he wore in Atlanta on his wedding day.

"I will, "John replied. "It'll be interesting to see just how many of them are left after Chickamauga. Just get things set up so Joanna can manage after you come back up, and oh, don't forget them damn rose bushes she wants, if that's what'll make her happy out there, but just remember there's a few other things that need tending to before ya'll start planting flowers."

The locomotive whistle sounded, prompting John to board, and with a belch of smoke and steam, the train left Elam. William reined Maggie and the wagon away from the station and over to William Stratton's General Merchandise, where the old tobacco chewing and spitting Yankee from Pomeroy in Meigs County, Ohio held a monopoly on the county's trade, his store being the only one in town. Stratton had seen the opportunity the railroad brought to North Georgia years before the war and had no qualms about coming south and being with Southerners to start a new venture. No one held his Northern origins against him since he was one of Mim County's original settlers and Elam's first and only merchant, and had a reputation for dealing fairly and generously with his customers even though he had no competition for miles around.

"Mornin' Mr. Stratton," William said, as he stepped inside and off the muddy main street. "Reckon I'm after something a little different today."

"Oh yeah," Stratton queried. "What's that?"

"I'm looking for roses to plant, need red ones, they must be red. Cousin John has brought a new bride from Atlanta...she's setting up housekeeping out at the place, and wants to put out roses like she had at home."

"Well, I'll be damned," Stratton exclaimed, raising his eyebrows and removing his spectacles. "That ornery cousin of yours got himself married; that's a bit of news to get around town. I'm surprised any woman would have him."

William had to crack a smile. "Yeah," he chuckled, "That's what I thought. Anyway...what about them roses?"

"Let's see, I think I've got some cuttings back there. How many do you need?" the storekeeper asked.

"Tell you what, I'll take them all off your hands, William said. "She'll need plenty to plant along the front of the porch."

As he left, he glanced over at a table where Stratton had stacked some newly arrived sun bonnets. William sorted through them, selecting a turkey-red flower print bonnet that he thought she might like, though he did not know what her favorite color was.

"Reckon I'll take this as well," he said. "She'll need something while she's working under the sun, if this blamed rain ever lets up."

"Yep," the women folk like a dash of color and pretty things," Stratton observed.

William had one more stop to make before he left Elam. John had instructed him to drop an envelope off at Lawyer Silas Moon's office, but had not told him what it contained...except to say that the contents were the 'insurance' to make sure his land and house would stay where he wanted it, in case he did not return from the war.

"Don't know what's in this, Mr. Moon, but John told me to make sure you had it" William said, as he gave it to the attorney.

He found Joanna out in front of the house when he returned, deciding where she wanted the roses planted. She smiled when she saw William arrive.

"Well, I found some roses down at Stratton's and got something else for you," William said, handing her the bonnet when he stepped down from the wagon.

"Why thank you, Cousin William," Joanna said. "I'll just tie this bonnet on and we'll get started getting my new roses in the ground."

William was mindful of John's reminder to get the important things done first, but he saw right away that Joanna had her mind set on rose planting, and that planting would cheer her up, so he went to the barn to find a pick and shovel.

October's remaining days went swiftly off the calendar, carrying him ever closer to the time when it would be his turn to travel on the train north back to the army. He made sure fences were mended, hay and forage was harvested and put up in the barn for the stock, and that the house and buildings were in shape for the coming winter, and of course, that Joanna's roses were planted. She made a good work partner, of course helping with the roses, but she assisted him with the other work John had charged him with.

As the autumn days grew shorter, the nights grew longer and snapped with chill. William was dutifully planning to sleep in the barn, figuring to be comfortable enough under a covering of hay and some warm quilts, but Joanna insisted that he stay in the house after darkness fell. She would retire to the bedroom while he made a pallet on the floor with the quilts in front of the hearth. She was John's wife and was beginning to get over her apprehension of being alone at the farm after he left. He admired her self-reliance and determination to make a life so far away from Atlanta, to uphold her obligation to her husband, but he was beginning to dread the day when he would have to say good-bye to her and leave her alone.

As the weeks passed, they had shared work, meals, thoughts, and dreams, dreams that were more alike as they grew to know each other. Though Joanna had not said so, bound by her vows to a man she was not sure of, she was dreading the day when William would be leaving, for she had become sure that he was a better man than her husband.

With the last week of the month a written summons arrived calling William back to the army and the morning came when she arose to find William in his uniform, with his blanket roll prepared for travel.

"If I leave a little before noon I'll get to town in time to catch the evening train," he told her. "I don't mind the walk in, can't see hitching up the wagon and riding in, leaving you to return with the wagon and the mule in the dark."

"You have done all you promised, Cousin William" Joanna said. "You have been a friend and a companion, and I for one wish the Army would let you stay home. John would be proud. I thank you and I will miss you. I hope you will find John well and I hope you and John will be safe and well. He has not written and I have no word of him since his return to the Army, and I want you to tell him to write and let his wife know how he is."

"I will do that Joanna. Stay safe, stay well and God willing we will all be back together soon. I will miss you too. Write to John, and I will see to it that he replies to you, although he's never been one to put down words on paper unless he felt he had to." William reached out and took her hand. "Farewell, Sister. I hope when I get back, those roses we planted will be blooming, maybe."

William shouldered his blanket roll, and began walking down Elam Road. Joanna waved goodbye. He had never called her 'Sister' before. She so wished this was the man she had married, and not John. She felt badly for her thoughts, and tried to think of other things.

As he disappeared down the road, limping slightly, she held the bonnet he had given her close to her heart, clutched it tightly, and said a silent prayer for his safe return.

Chapter 13

"Ain't nobody lived out here for a spell," Hascal Carter said, as they arrived at the house, and Lucille saw its white columned front for the first time, at the end of the dusty drive off Elam Road. The tobacco-spattered farmer had greeted her at the Elam depot in his dirty black farm truck after the hot, long train ride from Atlanta's Union Station.

"Reckon it's nice to have a visit from a big city cousin," Hascal smiled, showing his brown, tobacco stained teeth as he put her travel bag in the truck bed. "You Atlanta Carters ain't never paid us no heed before, so I got to wonder why you decided to come out here. Get ready for a dusty ride, the place is a few miles out; I went out yesterday and tried to make the place at least a little comfortable, but my guess is you won't be stayin' here long, story is, there's haints out there."

"Well, Cousin Hascal, I've always been interested in what happened around here during the War, especially what happened at Joanna and John's house," Lucille replied. "As for my lack of contact with your family, I was the one who cared for Ma Lavonia and that has taken all my time and effort and the years have gone by as we both know. She has passed now, and now I am free to visit, so here I am. I'm not afraid of 'haints', as you call them." She smiled as she slipped into the truck from the passenger's side.

"Yeah, well, I was sorry to hear about Lavonia, but of course none of us knew her, just knew of her," Hascal said. "It's quite a story, though, how old John fought them Yankees and then they killed him and his wife." He reached for his pouch of Beech Nut and cranked the truck motor. "But I say, let the dead bury the dead. I farm the land out there, but nobody wants to live in the house. My place is about two miles down the road. That's how strong them haint stories are, I reckon. I rented the house to a school teacher and his wife about a year ago, but they got out about a month later and moved to town."

It was a dusty ride, and a hot one, as Hascal promised.

"You need anything Cousin 'Cille, you just call," Hascal said, as he carried her bag to the front door and unlocked it. "Water's runnin'...I turned the phone and the power's back on. I stocked the ice box and the pantry with groceries, just hope you like what I put up for you, you can pay me back later."

"Thank you, Hascal, and the name is Lucille," she replied, surprised and mildly irritated that liberties had just been taken with her name by a person she had just met, even if he was a relative.

"Oh, OK, but you can call me Hass, I don't mind my name in short hand; never did like bein' called Hascal much," he replied. "Well, got to get back to the plowin', tryin' to get the bottom field ready next to the creek. So long for now."

She watched the red dust cloud the truck's wheels stirred up as it went up the drive and turned back onto Elam Road, and then she turned her attention to the roses. She had noticed them when she arrived, but now she saw the bright red blooms more closely. "How bright they are, and they're holding up well under this heat," she thought out loud to herself. "I wonder who cares for them."

Lucille walked the grounds before going inside and in back of the house was greeted by the shade of a solitary oak that spread its limbs over the graves of John and Joanna Carter. *"Maybe that's where the haunted legend began,"* she said to herself again as she viewed the headstones.

The sun had begun to set and bring dusk as she picked up her bag and entered the house. It had the look and scent of a place where no one had been in some time, and as she glanced to her right the wall mirror reflected the auburn haired, petite young woman she had become.

"You are like her", Ma Lavonia had said, looking up from her bed as she spent her final moments in the shadows of her bedroom. "You are like Joanna. I have never believed the story, the story of how she and John Carter died, never believed it," Lavonia whispered as her voice began to trail off. She held up her hand and grasped Lucille's, her grip surprisingly firm. "Go find the truth, girl, go find the truth about my sister child. There's nothing to hold you in Atlanta now, since I'll be gone. Go find out what happened to

Joanna...Joanna." With her sister's name on her lips, Lavonia Carter was gone.

Ma Lavonia was right about nothing to hold Lucille in Atlanta. With both her parents gone, killed in a car accident north of town two years ago, there was nothing to stop her from going to Mim County. She had stopped teaching third grade at Lena Mathis Elementary School so she could care for her grandmother, whether she would start teaching again somewhere, she did not know, but wondered if there was a possibility in Elam or Mim County if she decided to stay there.

Under her pale forehead her green eyes expressed her tiredness from the day, the train trip and then the dusty ride from Elam in Hascal's uncomfortable, soiled truck.

"Well, think I'll go freshen up, then see what Hascal put up for me in the kitchen", she said aloud once more to herself. After all, there was no one there to hear her. She was too tired to cook and snacked on sandwich bread and cheese she found in the refrigerator, and decided to unpack just enough to go to bed.

The summer thunderstorm swept in over the ridge and across the field in the predawn darkness, the sky born booming awakened Lucille from a fitful uncomfortable sleep in the stuffy, hot bedroom. She raised the window to hopefully catch a breeze, and now the curtains rustled as the wind and rain blew against the house and the cool air, though humid, brought relief. In the illumination of a lightning flash, a shadow appeared. It was a split second vision, that of a young woman, whose arm extended, pointing down at the travel trunk at the foot of the bed.

"Joanna, is that you, Joanna?" Lucille asked, but there was no reply, the vision lasting only as long as the lightning flash from the storm. Suddenly, the trunk lid rose and remained open.

Lucille peered down into it and the first thing she noticed was a faded, folded note dated June 20, 1864. The handwriting was clear and legible:

By my hand, this day, I have taken my husband's life.

By his own admission to me, he has taken my beloved William's life to make it appear he was killed by the enemy in battle.

By my hand, I have chosen not to live with the one who has slain my love. I will never bear your child, my sweet William, but I now free myself from a life that would be, for me, worse than death. May God forgive me. May God forgive us all. We will never lose each other.

Joanna Carter

It was cooler in the room now but Lucille could not sleep after reading Joanna's last words, and felt there was more in the trunk Joanna wanted her to see and so she began searching. Morning came with a knock at the door. It was Hascal Carter.

"Hey, Lucille, you in there," Hascal called out. "Got worried about you gal...was afraid them haints had carried you off. You all right?"

"I'm just fine Hascal, the haints, as you call them, did not carry me off," she replied. "As a matter of fact, I like it here...I've decided I want to stay, stay here quite awhile, and I want to tell you why. It all has to do with what happened to John and Joanna Carter. Hascal, the Yankees did not kill them. We need to have a long talk."

"Look Lucille, I ain't got time for a long talk, I still got a lot of plowin' to do down in the bottom section, and what do you mean, the Yankees didn't kill them?" Hascal replied, still standing in the doorway.

"You better take some time," Lucille said. "There are things you need to see, things you need to read, you're about to get a history lesson, a rather big one."

Lucille showed the reluctant farmer what she had found, the contents of the trunk, the letters that dispelled the story surrounding Joanna and John Carter and his cousin William. She showed him Joanna's last words which told how her husband really died, how his cousin really died, how she really died and why.

"Just what are you trying to pull here, woman," Hascal said, his eyes narrowing after reading the letters and messages. "You show up, and low and behold, all of a sudden, these letters and things just appear out of nowhere, telling of this scandal, this disgrace, about relations of mine who died

106

bravely for what they believed in. I don't believe any of it. They died fighting the Yankees and were killed by Yankee raiders when the war came to Mim County and this ain't gonna change it!"

"These letters have been in this house all along," Lucille said. "They tell the truth, these are real, I have not fabricated them, I just discovered them, and I can't believe no one up here knew about them and knew what they reveal, and Cousin Hascal, whether this changes things, well, that's up to you."

"What do you mean by that, I don't like your tone, lady," Hascal said, looking her in the eyes.

Lucille looked right back, making sure he knew her eyes met his. "I think it's time Mim County knew the truth about how John and Joanna died, and his cousin William," Lucille said. "It's a hell of a story really, of love, betrayal and murder, certainly a lot more exciting than people getting shot down in battle and shot down in their home by raiding cavalry, don't you think? Don't you think it's time to tell what really happened, and if you don't, what are you willing to do about it?"

Hascal blinked, cleared his throat, trying to find his words, but said nothing.

"With Ma Lavonia's dying breath she told me to come up here and find out what happened to her sister, that she never believed the story about the Yankee soldiers killing them," Lucille continued. "She, of course, did not know what was in Joanna's trunk, but somehow she knew or suspected the story she heard was not true. Well, it wasn't true, as it turned out, so I've accomplished my goal, kept my promise, but you know what Hascal, like I told you I like it here. It's peaceful and serene, and I have no reason to go back to Atlanta. I'm going to settle in right here, and Hascal, you're going to let me, aren't you."

Hascal was no longer looking Lucille in the eye, he was looking down sullenly. "Just what do you want?"

"I'm going to be the caretaker of the Carter House," Lucille said. "I will tend to the grounds, I will assume the responsibility of keeping the place up, it's a bit run down, you know. I'd like to restore it to its appearance when Joanna lived here. I teach, Hascal, I'm hoping to find a teaching position in Elam so I will of course pay you for staying here in addition to maintaining the property. It's really not a bad deal for you Hascal, you'll be getting more income out of this place than you ever have, and of course you'll continue to farm the land and oh, I want our agreement in writing, with both our signatures. That's not too high a price for perpetuating a legend that is a lie about your John Carter, the hero who was really a murderer."

Hascal looked down at the letters he had just read, spread across the kitchen table where Lucille had displayed them.

"From what I read looks like he had his reasons," Hascal said. "You know, when I first met you I warned you about the 'haints' out here. Hell, there's no need for you to worry, you're one of them."

"Oh, Cousin Hascal, if you knew, if you only knew," Lucille said, smiling.

Chapter 14

Kelsey Carter looked around the hardwood-paneled walls of Jim Taylor's law office waiting room and decided these were not his usual surroundings.

"Too rich for my blood, but that's going to change," he thought as he felt the tedium of expectation and apprehension grow and the room begin to close in on him. He wanted to see men with chain saws and back hoes and dump trucks busy at work on the property on Elam Road now that winter had finally loosened its grip, the snow and ice had melted and soaked into the earth, and the promise of spring and construction season had arrived. The realization of his dream was at hand.

In his mind, the big real estate sign to entice the home buyers was beside the road – "Carter Creek, a Place for Country Living", stood out in sharp outline against the cleared ground, empty of all the vestiges of the past he hated; that damned old house, those damned oak trees.

"Mr. Carter, Mr. Taylor will see you now," the secretary's voice interrupted Kelsey's vision, the real estate sign evaporated, replaced by his curiosity about why the attorney had called him.

Nothing could mess this up now, nothing will, by God," he mumbled as he walked in to find the attorney waiting for him behind his desk.

"Good morning Kelsey," Taylor's voice was overly friendly, arousing Kelsey's suspicion. "Have a seat... coffee? Alice just made a fresh pot."

"Done had all I need for today," Kelsey replied, flopping his bulk down into the stuffed leather chair in front of the desk. "So what's up, everything's ready to go ain't it?"

"We're not ready to close, Kelsey," Taylor replied, watching his unshaven, soiled client begin to scowl. "Got a call from Home Visions in Atlanta this morning; they want to talk to you."

"Talk, Hell! I'm ready to sell!" Kelsey exclaimed. "Thought you had all the closing papers drawed up...that you looked everything up, that everything was all set up!" What the hell do they want to talk about, and why did you pick now, of all times, to tell me?" "Dammit Taylor, you're supposed to be working for me!"

Taylor shifted in his chair and folded his hands as he leaned forward over his desk and cleared his throat. "Kelsey, on second thought, I think instead of coffee you might need a stiff drink of Jack Daniel's", he said. "There's no way to break this to you easily. You can't sell what you don't own. Yes, I did look everything up as you say; Kelsey, we have to look up everything, we have to determine who has clear title, who really owns what, and for how long, and this goes back a long, long time."

"I own that land, it's mine, passed down to me!" Kelsey yelled. The lawyer held up his hand. "Hear me out, Kelsey, just hear me out, you've got to know this," Taylor said. "This goes all the way back to the Civil War."

"The original owner of the land and the house was John Carter, killed along with his wife Joanna, by federal raiders back in 1864, when Sherman was invading Georgia. You ever hear of John Carter and his wife being killed by the Yankees? It's a famous story, Elam's claim to fame in that war, that and the battle that was fought out there."

"Yeah, I heard about all that, but I never paid much attention to history in school and I ain't in no mood for a damn history lesson now, Taylor!" Kelsey nervously replied. "You're beginning to sound like that damn cousin of mine, Willie Carter!"

"History is part of deed research, Kelsey," Taylor replied. "What land people owned, when they owned it; like it or not, sometimes what you find out is in your favor and sometimes it's not. Before John Carter left Mim County to fight in the Confederate Army, he deeded the land and house to his wife, Joanna. Guess he felt it would stay on his side of the Carter family if he got killed in battle, but it turns out it didn't, not on your side of the family, anyhow."

"It's ironic you refer to William Carter. He owns the house, the land, the creek that runs through it."

"I don't give a DAMN about any of that," Kelsey said. "All I've ever heard was my great, grand daddy Seborn owned the land, he passed it down to Granddaddy, he passed it down to Daddy, Daddy passed it down to me, I, by God, decided to sell it and that's all I care about Taylor! That's now, that's today, not no damn hundred odd years ago!"

"Kelsey, Seborn was John Carter's brother who thought it was John's land," Taylor replied. "That's what you and your family have assumed all these years, down through all these generations. I guess there was no reason, really, to question it, to check the records and deeds until you decided to sell. Obviously none of you knew about it. It's apparent John Carter never told anyone about deeding it to Joanna. Since John and Joanna were killed before they could have children, and since John deeded the land to her, it comes down to Lucille Carter."

Kelsey's scowl grew at the mention of Lucille Carter's name, and he began to shift in his chair as Taylor continued.

"Joanna's sister in Atlanta was Lucille's grandmother. They were a separate set of Carters and Joanna was a Carter before she married into the Mim County Carters through John. Lucille, who as you know died recently, moved to Mim County back in the 30's and Hascal Carter, your Dad, let her live in John and Joanna's house. I'm not clear on exactly why, but somehow shortly before she died, she found out about the deed and made out a will, leaving William Carter the property after learning she was Joanna's direct descendent."

Kelsey stared at the attorney but did not see him. His vision, his dream, his hope was vanishing. There would be no "Carter Creek" Subdivision, no money, no easy future, no respect, nothing.

"I'll have that shot of Jack Daniel's now," Kelsey said.

Taylor reached into his lower desk drawer for the bottle and a shot glass; Kelsey accepted it, belted down the whiskey and asked for another.

"Who knows about this besides you and me, right now," he asked. "Home Visions knows, Taylor replied. "I had to tell them, that's why they want to talk to you. They think you are trying to commit land fraud."

"What!!" Kelsey screamed, as he stood straight up, dropping the shot glass on the carpeted floor. "Just what kind of damn goat-roping is this Taylor?"

The attorney discreetly but quickly slid his chair back from the desk. "I explained all of that to them, Kelsey," Taylor said, nervously pouring more whiskey in another glass as he looked up at the angry man now towering over him.

"I feel sure we can work all that out before they decide to bring charges against you, that you are an unwitting victim of circumstance and bad fortune. Now sit down Kelsey, calm yourself down, and here, have another drink."

Kelsey accepted the full shot glass and gulped its contents down in one swallow, coughing as the liquor burned his throat.

"Does Willie Carter know about any of this," Kelsey asked with a rasping voice.

"No, but he's going to find out soon when the will is read" Taylor replied, hoping the Jack Daniel's would start having its effect soon.

"Damn!" was all Kelsey could muster. Just damn....Give me another drink."

Chapter 15

Lucille stepped in from the porch as the cold midwinter wind-swept the front of the house, giving her a chill. Dr. Lewis had advised her to stay inside and take her medicine and not go wandering about the property tending to things, especially the roses, now in their seasonal dormancy.

He did not want her to exert herself since her examination for chest pain a week ago, so she resigned herself to stay inside where it was warm and read.

It was not a pretty day outside anyway, with the sun hidden behind the clouds. To warm herself, she decided to fix a pot of hot tea, but suddenly, there was a faint rustling sound from the living room. Standing there was the same shadowy figure of a young woman she had seen so many years ago, that first night she spent in the house, the night she found the secrets that led to her many years in Mim County.

"Joanna, you have returned" Lucille said to the figure, but then, you have never really left here, have you?"

The shadow did not speak, but replied with a smile and pointed to the bookcase that for so many years had occupied its place across from the hearth.

An envelope with faded writing Lucille had never noticed before protruded from her book collection on the second shelf next to her copy of

Emily Dickinson poems. It was addressed to Joanna Carter from attorney Silas Moon and dated November 14, 1863. Lucille opened it. It was a legal notice that a change had been filed at the Mim County Courthouse naming Joanna as the owner of John Carter's property. Lucille looked up and the vision was gone.

Lucille read the document over and over, and wished she had known about this when she confronted Hascal Carter about what was in Joanna's trunk all those years ago. Recalling that Joanna was her grandmother Lavonia's sister, Lucille realized she was Joanna's only living relative. There was only one thing to do now. She had to go to Elam the next day for another doctor visit and a heart examination, but now she had a more important mission. She had to go to her lawyer...she had to make a will. The chest pains had become more frequent, and fearing she may not have much time left, she wanted Carter House, as she had come to call it, to be left to the one person she cherished and cared for more than anyone else, the young man who was the son she never had, Ellie's boy, William Carter.

Chapter 16

The house could still be seen easily through the bare oak tree limbs as William and Bobbie turned off Elam Road.

In a few weeks the limbs would fill out with new leaves and a visitor would have to move past them to see the columned front and Joanna's roses, now just beginning to bud and bloom in the early spring sunlight. Their full richness was still weeks away, but there were a few early blooms accenting the porch and the front steps.

"Oh, the roses," Bobbie said, smiling as she got out of the car. "Her roses are beginning to bloom, only now they are your roses, William."

"No, they are still hers," he replied. "They always will be. Joanna's, then Aunt Cille's and now mine, I guess," William replied. "Aunt 'Cille always made me feel like I belonged here, all those summer days I spent out here."

"And now you do," Bobbie said. "Now you can save this place, preserve this house, this ground, these trees, these roses. Mim County may change all around here, but this place will remain. I am so glad, and so proud."

"Thank you," William said. "I'm glad you are here, that you came with me out here."

The sun, now arching over the oak trees, caught the shimmer of Bobbie's hair, and he took her hand.

"If I was a history teacher, and you were a lady, would you marry me anyway, would you have my baby" he asked.

Bobbie laughed. "Well, aren't you the song writer!!...only you stole those lyrics from Bobby Darrin! I'll have you know, William Carter, that you are a history teacher and I am a lady, and yes, yes, God, oh yes, I will marry you and I want to have your baby. I want to be with you for the rest of our lives, wherever you go, wherever you are, I will be with you, but I hope you decide to be here, and instead of the hatred and death and heart break that was once here, we will have love and peace. I love you, William Carter, I love you so much and I always have."

They walked to the rear of the house where the fading headstones marked the graves of John and Joanna. William gazed across the pasture behind them, he thought of the creek and the woodland beyond the ridge where the men of Elam and Mim County, the men of Company 'G' had withstood the federal cavalry and artillery assault.

"They buried the men from Elam where they fell after the battle," William said. "They were re-interred later in the town cemetery, but they never found William Carter. He's still back there somewhere."

"Shouldn't people know what really happened here that day, how Joanna and John and William really died," Bobbie asked?

"We know the true story the letters and Joanna's final words tell...the story Aunt 'Cille wanted you to know... and why Hascal Carter agreed to let her stay here"

"That was quite an agreement they drew up and signed wasn't it," William said. "Aunt Lucille put it in the trunk too, and old Hascal went to his grave holding onto the story that John Carter was a hero when he really murdered his cousin and got killed in return for the deed by his wife, who then ended her life. You know Bobbie, in a way, he murdered Joanna too, I think. He took away from her the one person who meant more to her than life itself. I think what is important is that I know the truth, and that you know it with me."

William knelt down and touched Joanna's headstone.

"As for Elam and Mim County, and history, well, the legend has become history here, and I think maybe the legend should stand as long as the people who really matter know what really happened. Since I am a historian I guess that's a hell of a thing for me to say, but that's how I feel. There is one change I want to make here. I want to erect a headstone for William next to Joanna's."

The old oak cast its late afternoon shade across the yard and on the gravestones.

You know, I really think Joanna and William would like that," Bobbie said, taking William by the arm. "Well, William Carter, what say we go have our first supper together in this new possession of yours, and then, our first night together where we're going to spend the rest of our lives."

Three hours before dawn, William and Bobbie held each other close, watching and listening as a thunderstorm hurled its lightning down. Suddenly a crash in the rear yard shook the house and the sky roared angrily above the roof.

"We'll wait until daylight, and check around for any damage," William said. "That was very close, I wonder if it struck the oak out in back."

"Well, I don't think I can get back to sleep," Bobbie replied, still holding William. He rose and hastily dressed.

"I don't know how, but I think the power is still on. I'm going to look around the house and go ahead and put on some coffee."

"I'm going with you," Bobbie said.

The storm's devastation greeted them as the morning light came over the ridge. The rear yard oak tree's overhanging limb that had for so long shaded the graves was splintered and shorn off. Beneath it lay the shattered, broken pieces of what had been John Carter's headstone. Joanna's gravestone stood untouched, just out of reach of the fallen limb. On the ground next to it lay a fresh rose, crimson and moist, where William Carter's marker would be placed.

About the Author

Gerald Harding Gunn was born in Atlanta, Georgia. He is a career broadcast and website journalist. He is the proud father of two daughters, Olivia and Sarah. He currently resides in Gainesville, Georgia.

Gerald is an avid Civil War buff. His interest in the Civil War grew from a visit to the Cyclorama at the age of seven. He has participated in living histories and reenactments off and on since he was fifteen. His main focus is on the Atlanta Campaign which is the setting for his book, "*A Rose for William Carter*".

Jerry, as he prefers to be called, is also co-author of the novel **"Ghosts of Kennesaw Mountain"** along with Lois Helmers.

We hope you enjoyed this wonderful story as much as we did. For more great stories please visit our web site at:

www.BadgleyPublishingCompany.com